TWO RAVENS

TWO RAVENS

CECELIA HOLLAND

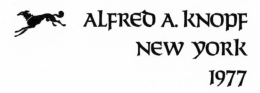 ALFRED A. KNOPF
NEW YORK
1977

VT

THIS IS A BORZOI BOOK
PUBLISHED BY ALFRED A. KNOPF, INC.

Library of Congress Cataloging in Publication Data

Holland, Cecelia, [date]
Two ravens.

I. Title.
PZ4.H733TW [PS3558.0348]   813'.5'4   76–49833
ISBN 0–394–49988–3

Manufactured in the United States of America

FIRST EDITION

To the memory of my grandmother

PART ONE

THERE WAS A FARMER named Hoskuld, who lived in the west of Iceland, who was called Walking Hoskuld because he was so tall no horse could carry him. By a handfast marriage he had a son whose name was Bjarni. One day while they were cutting driftwood Bjarni said that he wanted to leave Iceland.

His father put the axe down head to the ground and stared at him. "Where did you have in mind to go?"

"Vinland. Or Norway."

"Well, you'd better choose between them, you fool, they're in two opposite directions."

Bjarni reached for his own axe and set to chopping at the log at his feet. Hoskuld was still. Bjarni could feel his gaze on him.

"That's my thanks," Hoskuld said, "for fathering you in the first place and feeding you thereafter. Now when you are big enough to help me, you will walk away without a look back."

Bjarni said, without stopping in the work, "Ulf can help you." Ulf was Hoskuld's second son.

"Ulf! Ulf does nothing except dream about women."

Bjarni chopped through the log so hard the two pieces

flew up off the sand. He picked up the wood and carried it to the cart fifty feet away.

When he came back, his father was still staring at him. "Why?"

Bjarni stooped for his axe. Hoskuld gripped him by the shoulders of his shirt and yanked him back up.

"Why?"

They were face to face; there was no difference between them in height. Bjarni said nothing. Hoskuld slapped his cheek.

"Answer me!"

Bjarni slapped him back as hard as he could. "That's an answer."

Hoskuld seized his axe. Bjarni set himself, his fists raised between them. At length Hoskuld laid his axe back on his shoulder.

"Small thanks a man gets from his children these days. In the old days it was different." He walked down the beach. Bjarni followed him, wary. He did not turn his back on Hoskuld the rest of the day.

It was summer, and the light stayed in the sky from sundown to sunrise. They took the cart back through the hayfields to the farm their family had worked for two hundred years. The path climbed the hill toward the buildings, half a mile away. Above the homestead the slope turned steeper, and at its top the rock cliff burst out of the green grass and stood up hundreds of feet sheer into the sky; on this rock cliff the ravens nested, and so the farm was called Hrafnfell, the Raven Roost.

The six farm buildings below the cliff were sunk halfway

down into the ground, the aboveground walls built of lava blocks, and the whole roofed over with sod. Besides Bjarni and his father, Hoskuld's three other sons lived there, and his wife and his stepson. On the hill above the buildings was the woodyard. Bjarni and Hoskuld unloaded the wood they had taken from the beach and stacked it.

As they led the horses and cart into the yard below, the cookhouse door opened, and Hoskuld's wife came out. She carried a round basket of bread in one arm and the mead jug in the other. Her name was Hiyke. Bjarni watched her pass by him. She was Hoskuld's third wife, much younger than he, only seven years older than Bjarni: Hoskuld saw him with his eyes on her and swore.

"That's why!" He had a bridle in his hand; he whipped it at Bjarni's head. Bjarni caught the leathers and pulled the bridle out of his father's hand.

Hiyke was watching them. "Do you never tire of it?" she said to Hoskuld. "What are you fighting about now?"

"See she does not find out," Hoskuld said to Bjarni. He took the jug in his right hand and his wife's arm in his left and went into the hall. Bjarni took the horses into the barn and tended to them; he did not go into the hall that evening.

WHEN THE SUN ROSE above the cliff Bjarni brought in the goats to be milked. He tethered them in the barn and watered them. Climbing the ladder to the loft, he lay down on his back in the straw and made poems in his head. Below, the barn door creaked. His stepmother came in to milk the goats.

The wit for poetry left him. He lay still in the deep straw listening to Hiyke directly below him. She spoke humorously to the goats. Presently the jets of milk began to play into the bucket. Bjarni rolled over onto his stomach. Carefully he pushed the straw aside. Through the chink between the boards of the loft he looked down on her.

Her hair was black. He had spent long hours here thinking of ways to describe it but all his words failed him. She wore it pulled tight over her head and braided, and the braids coiled over her ears.

His brother Ulf came into the shed, yawning, his fair hair shaggy. "Is Bjarni here?"

"I have not seen him," Hiyke said.

Bjarni said nothing, loathe to let her know that he had been watching her. She held the bucket between her knees as she milked; the goat took a step away and Hiyke spoke to it. Ulf was coming up behind her, which had startled the goat.

"Give me a sup of the milk," he said.

"Keep your hands off the milk," she said.

"Have you not seen Bjarni? He must be here." Ulf walked away from her, toward the ladder. In the loft, Bjarni pulled the straw over the chink in the boards and rolled onto his back.

Ulf came up the ladder. "Ho," he called. "What are you doing up here?" He strode across the loft, stooping under the rafters. He was a big man, although not so tall as Bjarni.

"What do you want?" Bjarni said to him.

"I thought you were going to Eirik Arnarson's." Ulf came down on one knee beside him.

Bjarni rested his head on his arms. "Hoskuld is right," he said to his brother. "All you think about is women."

"Who said anything of women?" Ulf said, smiling.

"Why else would you go to Eirik Arnarson's?"

Ulf laughed his roaring laugh. "Are you up here dreaming about vikings?"

Bjarni went over to the ladder and started down it into the bottom of the shed. Hiyke passed by him, carrying the pail of milk toward the door. He tore his gaze away from her.

"Why are you going to Eirik Arnarson's?" she said. She put down the pail and lifted her shawl over her head.

He muttered something and took the pail from beside her feet. The door hung open. He walked into the brilliant sunshine.

BJARNI AND ULF went off around the bay toward the farm where their chieftain Eirik Arnarson lived, up on the northern shore. Ulf rode his grey mare and Bjarni walked. Eirik Arnarson's farm was less than five miles away over the water, but the walk around the bay took them into the afternoon.

The chieftain's home was set in the shelter of a hillside. A wall of lava chunks surrounded the buildings. Ulf tied his mare's reins to the gate. Bjarni asked at the

hall and was told that Eirik had gone up the hill to over-
see the haying.

Ulf had gone indoors. Bjarni followed the path up the
hill. The hayfield was on the lee above the farmhouses.
The three workmen had cut the hay and were going
through the field raking it up into mounds. On the high
side of the field, the chieftain sat on his horse watching.
When he saw Bjarni he raised his hand and shouted a
greeting.

The wind was blowing steadily off the ocean. Bjarni
climbed up into it as he crossed the slope. He shook
hands with Eirik and they said the usual things. Eirik
called to one of his men. Bjarni stood back to let them
talk. Over the ridge to the west that sheltered the hayfields lay the broad ocean. To the east the cinder mountains began, treeless and streaked with ice. Bjarni squinted,
straining his eyesight, to catch a glimpse of the glacier.

Eirik rode by him. Bjarni went along at his stirrup,
and they started down the hill.

When they were down in the lee of the hill Eirik
turned to him. "Bjarni Hoskuldsson, I'm very glad to
see you. What brings you here?"

"That which we spoke of at the Thing," Bjarni said.
"I have talked to Hoskuld, and he is interested. We will
buy half a shipload of timber the next time you send a
fleet to Vinland."

Eirik stroked his beard with his fingers. "What did
your father say about the price?"

"My stepmother's loom is far-famed. We have several
hundreds of her cloth."

"For a shipload I shall need ten hundreds, and that is only because your family and mine go back so far together."

"Half a shipload," Bjarni said.

"That will leave half a shipload unsold."

Bjarni shook his head. "Half a shipload only. I am not a merchant. All I want is wood to use on Hrafnfell."

"Hoskuld might think differently."

"Perhaps. He usually leaves such things to me."

"Yes, he is wise to do so. Have you considered the other thing we talked of at the Althing?"

At the Council of Iceland he had offered Bjarni work in his trade with Vinland. Bjarni said, "I have thought of it—I don't want you to think I would pass over it lightly—"

"But you will not take it."

"I don't have my father's permission yet to leave home."

"Permission!" Eirik Arnarson said. "Just go."

Bjarni said nothing to that. They were coming to Eirik's yard. The chieftain leaned forward suddenly in his saddle. He had seen the grey mare at the gate.

"Did you come here alone? Your brother Ulf came with you, didn't he?" He shouted to his horse and galloped away.

Bjarni followed him into the yard. Eirik rushed into the hall. In a few moments Ulf appeared in the loft window of the hall and jumped down to the ground. His shirt was unlaced and he had his belt in his hand. He hurried toward Bjarni, who went to the grey and untied her reins.

Eirik came out of the hall again.

"I told you to stay away from her! By Christ my Judge, if I find you with her again—"

Ulf jumped onto the mare's back. Bjarni went ahead of him out the gate.

"Don't come back," Eirik shouted. "I will take a whip to you, you horse-eating pagan pig!"

"You might try, Cross-kisser," Ulf said.

"I'll thrash you bloody-backed!"

"Old man, you talk too much!"

Bjarni led the mare by the bridle onto the path. He raised his hand to Eirik Arnarson. The chieftain did not answer his wave.

BETWEEN EIRIK ARNARSON'S FARM and Hrafnfell on the south shore of the bay were four other farms. Hoskuld had a fishing ship called *Swan;* from these other four farms came men to crew her. They sailed out onto the ocean and searched for the cod, swimming in schools of thousands off Iceland.

Hoskuld found the cod by the whales and grampuses feeding on them. He stood in the stern of his ship, with the spoke of the steerboard braced against his thigh, and shouted to the oarsmen to hold. Bjarni sat at his bench in the stern just forward of his father. A wave lifted the ship up high and he looked across the broad grey sea. Half a mile away the cod-whales were basking on the surface, but the sun was under clouds.

Hoskuld tramped down the spine of the ship. "There's a good risk of fog. We'll try the net. Bjarni and I will tow it out." In the bow, his younger sons were already hurrying to put out the small boat. They did not move fast enough for Hoskuld, who swore at them and kicked them. Bjarni shipped his oar.

"Keep the boat between you and Papa," Ulf said softly. He had the bench just in front of Bjarni.

On *Swan*'s lee side, the other men were lowering the long roll of the net down over the rail. Hoskuld was leading the ship's boat back toward the stern. Bjarni stood up, his knees bent to help him keep his balance, and when the wave brought the boat up to the ship's rail, he stepped across into it. Hoskuld came after him.

"Row her," Hoskuld said. He went into the stern. With one hand he directed Bjarni here and there over the waves, until he could reach the tail end of the rolled net.

They stretched the net out and opened it up so that *Swan* could drag it through the water. As they worked, Hoskuld said, "What did Eirik Arnarson say to you?"

Bjarni leaned back against the oars. The boat swooped sideways down a wave. "What I told you, about the wood. But we have not settled the price."

"Didn't you talk to him about going to Vinland? Hold, damn you!"

Hoskuld leaned over the stern to tend the net. Bjarni dropped his oars into the sea to hold the boat steady. He wiped his streaming face on his sleeve.

"He offered me that, yes."

"What did you tell him?"

"That I did not have your permission."

Hoskuld straightened. The rope of the float was coiled at his feet. It paid out after the net so fast it hopped on the stern rail. Hoskuld sat down sideways on the thwart.

"He made light of that—didn't he? The Christians—they have no sense of obligations."

"I am not obliged to row you all the way back to the ship," Bjarni said.

"No hurry." His father dropped the white float over the side. "Would you go to Vinland if I allowed it?"

"Give me your permission to leave, and I will decide what to do." Bjarni jabbed with his chin at the ship. "We are drifting off fast." A green wave rose between the boat and *Swan*, and the ship disappeared.

"I'll do what I can to help you," Hoskuld said. "But not to go to Vinland and fell trees."

Bjarni butted his oars together. The waves lifted them up again and the boat swooped down the crest of the water. The two men eyed each other. Finally Bjarni said, "You were unwilling, before."

"I have given it some thought." Hoskuld put his feet on the right side of the thwart and ran his oars out. "Row."

They rowed the boat back upwind to *Swan*. Nothing more was said between them. Hoskuld went back to *Swan*'s stern to take the tiller. Bjarni made the small boat fast in the bow of the ship and went aft to his bench.

The other men had rigged the lines to the net. They sat down to their oars, and Hoskuld called their orders. Bjarni wiped his hands on his thighs and took hold of his oar. Ulf sat just in front of him. When the net began to weigh Ulf would come back and share Bjarni's oar.

Hoskuld cried, "Pull!"

The eighteen oars swooped down to meet the sea. Bjarni put his back into the stroke. At first the oar resisted, the water clung to the ship, but slowly *Swan* glided forward. She lightened; her rigging began to whine.

Something moved at the fringe of Bjarni's vision. He looked in time to see one of the net-lines loop around the haft of the axe, set there in case the line fouled.

"Hoskuld!" Bjarni cried. The tightening line jerked the axe up over the rail of the ship, and Bjarni dove after it.

The cold sea met him. The axe was falling away through the darkening green water. With a stroke of his arms he cut through the water and caught hold of the axe.

He bobbed up to the surface again. *Swan* was gone; all he could see was the water piling up before him in a white-capped wave. A line sliced the side of the wave. He swam awkwardly after it, with the axe weighting him down.

The wave fell away under him. *Swan* was just beyond. Bjarni pulled himself along the net-line back to the ship. All the men on that side reached down their arms to him. Hoskuld left the tiller and fell on Ulf.

Ulf yelped. Hoskuld struck him full on the face with his open hand.

"What are you hitting him for?" Bjarni shouted. "It was Jon and Andres who set the lines." He swung the axe up and handed it to a man above him in the ship.

Hoskuld straightened, letting Ulf go. He cast a broad look around the ship. "Grampus," he said. "Get back into the ship." Stepping from bench to bench, he went forward, where his younger sons were standing up in their places.

Bjarni put his hands on the rail of the ship and vaulted out of the water. The icy wind flattened his shirt against his body. Ulf lifted off the top of the bench and took out a bearskin. Bjarni wrapped himself in it. A hundred yards away a fin sheared the water. When the grampus turned, the sun shone on its white side under the water.

Jon was arguing with Hoskuld; a crack of a blow stopped him. Bjarni sat down on the bench. He watched the grampus circle past the ship again.

The deck shivered under his feet; Hoskuld was coming back. His knuckles were bleeding. He stood before Bjarni and said, "You call me *father*."

"Nothing could make me admit it," Bjarni said.

Hoskuld's chest swelled, and his small mean eyes glittered like spear-points. He said, "Did you save the axe?"

Bjarni showed him the axe. His father said, "Be glad," and went past him to the steerboard.

On the bench in front of Bjarni's, Ulf sat nursing a split lip. There was blood all over his chin. Bjarni clapped him on the shoulder.

"Stiffen up."

"I hate to fish," Ulf said. He turned to his oar. Behind them, Hoskuld lifted his voice.

"Pull!"

WHEN THEY HAD TAKEN as many fish as the ship could hold, they sailed back to the bay of Hrafnfell. There the women of the farms split the fish and hung them up on frames to dry in the sun. The men cleaned the ship and spread out the nets and mended them.

Hoskuld called for his jug and the chessboard. He sat down on the grass where a boulder blocked the wind and told Bjarni to play chess with him.

Bjarni sat on his heels on the opposite side of the board. They passed the jug back and forth as they played. Hoskuld took three drinks to Bjarni's two. Bjarni won the game, but Hoskuld stayed jovial.

"Here." He put the jug over on Bjarni's side of the board. "Get drunk. Maybe then I'll beat you. Have you thought over what I told you?"

"What—that I can go anywhere but Vinland?"

"I have an old friend who lives in the Hebrides. Sigurd Gormsson is his name. He needs men. It's rougher work than felling timber for Eirik Arnarson."

"Fighting?"

"Well, what comes up."

Bjarni fingered a black pawn. On the beach the wind stirred the racks of drying fish like silver leaves. A boy was running up the slope toward the chessplayers. Bjarni looked down at the chesspiece in his hand. The boy reached them, out of breath: Kristjan, Hoskuld's stepson, Hiyke's son.

"Shall we anchor the ship out in the bay now? We are done with her."

"Haul her up onto the beach," Hoskuld said. He pushed his finger into Kristjan's face. "Tell them if her hull sees a rock I'll mend their beards into the nets."

Kristjan ran off. His black hair tossed on his shoulders. Among the women on the beach, among the racks of fish, his mother might be watching him.

"The Hebrides," Bjarni said. "That's away over the sea. How am I to get there?"

Hoskuld smiled at him. "I will take you there. In *Swan*." He put out both hands for the jug.

The Hebrides Islands were far to the south, a long, complicated sail. Bjarni said, "How would you know how to get to the Hebrides?" Yet he knew of old rumors about Hoskuld, a murder, an exile spent aviking.

His father said, "I'm not surprised you hesitate. I myself was somewhat younger than you when I sailed, but times were different then." He pulled on the jug and smacked his lips, wiping his beard with his fingers, smiling at Bjarni. "Maybe you should stay here, and start calling me *father*."

"I will go," Bjarni said.

Hoskuld handed the jug to him. Bjarni thought, He is glad to be rid of me. While he raised the jug to drink, he looked down the slope toward the women, hanging up the fish in the sun.

IN THE LATE AFTERNOON Bjarni climbed over the hillpath that led to the ocean and came to the hot springs. He stripped off his clothes and walked into the pool. At first the waist-deep water was icy cold. He stepped into a sulphurous eddy and a ribbon of heat curled around his legs. He sank down to his neck in the water.

The north wind was blowing hard. Rain was coming. From the spring he could look down through a notch between two slopes of the hill and see the ocean in the distance. Catching the axe in the sea had been lucky. Thor was with him. Whatever Hoskuld intended with his sudden friendship, in the end it would all happen according to fate anyway. He was glad that he had named Thor first at the Sacrifice on Midsummer's Day. The hot water soaked the ache out of his muscles. He sank down entirely under the water and swept his hair back with his hands.

When he put his head up to the air again, a pebble rattled down the trail behind him. A footstep crunched. He turned and saw Hiyke coming down the steep path toward him.

She came up to the edge of the spring. "This is a foolish, mad thing Hoskuld is planning. You are a grown man. Can't you leave home by yourself?"

"He wants to go."

"Would you change your mind if I told you that he is plotting some wickedness?"

He frowned at her. *"Some wickedness?"*

"He said you would never come back again."

She was standing at the foot of the path, her grey shawl over her head and shoulders and the ends crossed over her breast. A silver cross hung around her neck on a chain. Her skin was fine and pale as parchment, her face shaped hollow over the frail bones. He thought over what she had told him.

"He is a vile man," he said. "Why do you stay with him?"

That angered her. She started back up the path, her skirts in her hands. Over her shoulder, she flung words at him.

"Vile enough to father you, you shiftless lout. Get to the Hebrides in your own way."

She went foot above foot up the path. He watched her from the sour water until she disappeared over the hill.

HOSKULD WENT over the mountains to another part of Iceland. Bjarni and Ulf fitted the ship *Swan* out for the voyage. Throughout two long days of rain Bjarni laid out all the cordage and sails; he worked so hard he did not stop to eat or drink.

"Why are you in such a hurry?" Ulf said. "We can't leave until Father comes back."

They were stowing away the sails in the bow. The deck awnings were rigged over the beached ship; rain drummed on the canvas. Bjarni shut the sail locker.

"What if we did?" he said to Ulf.

His brother's breath hissed between his teeth. "Go without him. Is that what you mean?"

"You and I are good sailors. We can take Hoskuld's maps and sun-wheel." Crouched down under the awning, Bjarni walked on bent legs back to the waist of the ship, where the awning opened. Ulf followed him. They jumped down to the gravel. The wind swept the long raindrops at them.

Ulf gripped Bjarni's arm. His face glowed red with excitement. "You mean to take Father's ship?"

"What do you think?"

"Let's do it. Oh, let's do it."

They went up the slope toward the farm buildings. The grass was littered with thunderstones thrown out of the volcanoes. The wind keened on them. Bjarni kept his face down out of the rain. He wondered if there was anywhere else in the world like Hrafnfell. Ahead of Ulf he went in the door to the hall and down the three steps.

The hall was much longer than it was wide. An open hearth ran down the middle of it. Only the logs at the far end were burning, where the table was and the High Seat. Bjarni and Ulf went down the room toward it.

The High Seat was covered with a bearskin. Hiyke was Christian; she kept the black fur draped over the whole of the double chair, to hide the carvings on it. Jon and Andres were sitting at one side of the table, playing chess. No one else was in the hall. Bjarni put his hands on the table and leaned on his arms, his eyes on his younger half brothers.

"I am sailing tomorrow in *Swan* for the Hebrides. Are you coming with me?"

At once the two young men stood up in their places. Andres said, "Without Papa? What do you mean?" and Jon said at the same time, "Papa would flog us when we came back."

The door slammed at the other end of the hall. Bjarni glanced over his shoulder. Down the dark hall Kristjan was coming toward them, Hiyke's half-grown son.

Bjarni turned to his half brothers again. "I don't mean to come back. Hoskuld's friend in the Hebrides will welcome me much better if I bring a ship and its crew with me, even a little ship like *Swan*."

"That's stealing," Andres said. "It's Papa's ship."

Long-faced, and with his hands in his sleeves, Kristjan joined them. He was slight and dark, a changeling among the tall fair Hoskuldssons. He said, "You are stealing Hoskuld's ship?"

"Yes," Jon said. "I'll go. I hope I never see this place again, too. Or Papa."

"That's well wished," Ulf said.

"It's stealing," Andres said. "It's stealing."

"It was Hoskuld's notion," Bjarni said. "In part."

The door opened again at the other end of the hall and a step squealed. The men hushed their voices. Hiyke came toward them; she carried a basket on her hip. In their midst she stopped and looked from face to face.

"What is this, now? You look like the bishops arguing over a *filioque*."

Bjarni said, "We are sailing tomorrow."

She put the basket down on the table and stepped up to him. "You mean that you are robbing us." She spoke straight into his face. "That is vile, is it not?"

"If you call it so," he said. "I see no other way, aside from killing him."

"Bah." She jerked away from him. Kristjan stood off to one side, alone. She said to him, "And you, good-for-nothing—you are going, too?"

"I can do anything they can do," Kristjan said.

She walked away from them, going straight out of the hall. Ulf twitched back the napkin over the basket and a steamy fragrance rose from the bread stacked inside.

JUST BEFORE DAWN, the firebell began to clang. Bjarni was sleeping in the loft of the barn. Barefoot, his shirt unlaced, he jumped down to the yard. The bell sounded in his ears.

"The ship!" Ulf ran out of the sleeping booth, pulling on his shoes. "The ship is on fire!"

Bjarni sprinted down toward the bay. The sky was white with sunlight. The, longship lay on its gunwale on the beach above the tide line. The canvas awning was all afire. Flames towered up out of the hold. He knew Hiyke had set it, to keep them there.

Jon was already there, and was throwing water onto the

fire from a little bucket. Bjarni reached the ship. The canvas was burnt away; fire billowed through the whole long hull. The ship was packed with straw. It was the straw that burned. Bjarni gripped the oar rail. The wood was heating from the fire.

"Help me! Jon—"

He flung his weight against the rail. Jon and Ulf sprang to help him. They rocked the ship up off her side onto her flat keelboard and skated it down the gravel beach. Other men reached them from the farm. They drove *Swan* down to meet the low waves of the bay.

"Swamp her," Bjarni cried. Up to his knees in the water, he dragged *Swan* forward until he felt her floating. He pushed down with all his strength on the oar rail, and the ship rolled over.

The fire drowned with a hiss. The men stood back from the hull, barely afloat in the bay's soft waves. Swatches of charred straw fouled the water. They swam the overturned ship out into deeper water and turned her rightside up again.

Bjarni waded toward the beach. In the shallows he passed by Ulf and Andres; he said, "Haul her in and see how badly she is hurt." Without pausing he walked out of the water and climbed the slope toward the buildings.

The sheep were clipping the grass around the black thunderstones. In tight bunches they hurried out of his way, their heads back. He went straight through the farmyard and into the hall.

Hiyke was just stepping down from a stool she had

put below the window; she had watched it all. He went across the room to her.

"You did that," he said. "You burned the ship."

"I would happily die," she said, "if the funeral would keep you from leaving." Her low voice trembled. "You are taking everything. It is not just—you will leave us with nothing—"

As she argued she put out her hands, and he caught hold of her wrists. She twisted her arms to free herself. He held her fast. She gave a low cry, half of pain. He pulled her to him and kissed her.

She fought. He pressed his mouth tight over her mouth. He held her close against him, both muffled in their clothes; he stroked his hand down over her loins. The door behind them banged open.

"Mother!"

Bjarni put her down. Wheeling, he faced her son coming down the room. Kristjan stopped still. He cast around him for a weapon and picked up the fire-iron from the hearth.

"Leave my mother alone."

Wary of the fire-iron, Bjarni went toward him, his hands out. Kristjan tongued his lips. His eyes darted here and there. He stood fast until Bjarni was almost on him and then scurried backward down the hall, to his mother.

"Go," she said; she took the fire-iron from Kristjan's hands. "I will manage this."

"Mother—"

Bjarni straightened, his arms falling to his sides. Over

the black fire-iron he met her fierce unflinching gaze. She thrust her head at Kristjan.

"Go on—go out."

Kristjan bolted up the steps and out the door. Bjarni said, "Hiyke, listen to me."

"Take the ship," she said. "Take everything you want. Take them all with you. I hope I never set eyes on you again."

She moved out of his way, the iron raised between them. He went out of the hall.

THE SHIP WAS NOT BURNED; only the straw and the canvas had burned. They laid out fresh canvas for sails and new line for the rigging. The next day rain began to fall again. Bjarni could wait no longer; Hoskuld would be back soon. With Ulf he went up onto the headland above the ocean, at the mouth of the bay. On the rocks there he cut runes to charm the ship and its crew, to keep great Thor's kindness on himself.

Ulf sat in the lee of the rock, grumbling. He had his coat over his head to protect him from the rain.

"We should go. Why are you wasting time here?"

The soft rock yielded to Bjarni's knife. It gave off a faint ashy smell. He kept the lines straight and even; ill-made runes brought bad luck. "You sound like a Christian," he said.

"I don't see much difference between your magic and theirs."

Ulf was devout in nothing. Bjarni wiped his wet hand on his thigh. His gaze traveled the three lines of runes.

Hammerer
Keep safe the White Raven
Her naked nestlings

At the bottom he wrote:

Guard Hoskuld's son

If Hoskuld came here and found the runes he would not mar them, since they carried his own name.

"I'm never coming back here," Ulf murmured. "Never again. Never."

"I am finished," Bjarni said.

They went in single file back down the thread of path, traveling the high edge of the cliff above the sea. Far below was the beach where the men of Hrafnfell cut driftwood for the fire. Ulf bundled his head and shoulders in his coat against the rain. Bjarni walked with his head hunched down. He turned his face inland, out of the rain. He looked over the bowl of the valley around the bay. Shreds of mist clung to the higher slopes, and the clifftops were lost in cloud. Never coming back. He dragged his gaze from Hrafnfell. The rain blew into his face.

They went straight down the hillside. There was no need to go back to the buildings; all their gear was stowed away in the ship, at anchor just beyond the breakers. The heads of the other Hoskuldssons and Kristjan showed above the oar rail. They would not get far today, in the rain. Still it would be far enough. Bjarni lengthened his stride toward them.

HOSKULD HAD MEANT to swell his crew with men from the neighboring farms. Because Bjarni was not coming back to Iceland he had to sail along the coast from farm to farm, asking at each place for sailors, until he found oarsmen enough.

Swan carried nine oars to the side. When he had eighteen men aboard, he filled the watercask amidships and turned the bow of the ship to the east, to row out of the strong current that stirred the sea around Iceland. The weather had cleared. In a sunny dawn they raised the sail and put Iceland behind them over the horizon.

Bjarni had his father's sun-wheel and two charts. By the sun-wheel he could tell his northing, but he had no way of finding *Swan's* position by east and west. The sun set for only a few moments each night, and the sky never darkened enough to steer well by the stars. Therefore Bjarni determined to sail as far as possible within sight of land. He sailed due east; he followed Hoskuld's chart and measured the height of the sun with Hoskuld's wheel. On the second day after Iceland slid into the sea behind them, a mountainous coast loomed up over the eastern line. The chart foretold it; Bjarni began to trust it.

A north wind was blowing. *Swan* ran before it with the mountains of Norway just in sight to the east. High-spirited, the Icelanders nagged and argued with Bjarni to sail in to Norway; they pictured it stocked with loose women and heaped with treasure. Bjarni tended the chart, marking down everything he saw: the color of the sea, the flights of birds. The chart said that he would raise islands in the southwest by sailing down this coast. His eyes turned constantly toward the horizon.

The islands appeared on the third day after they turned south. He sailed *Swan* down past them and stood out to the southwest, and other islands pricked up into the sky farther south. The chart said that he could follow these islands to the Hebrides.

"In the old days," Ulf said, "we would have carried shields on our benches, and that would have been a serpent's head." He pointed to the curled prow of the ship.

They talked of Eirik Bloodaxe and the raids of Hastein and Harald Hardrada. Jon and Andres came back into the stern benches to listen. Later Kristjan joined them, off by the edge of them, as he always was. Bjarni was cutting runes into the blade of his oar, and Ulf told stories.

After a while, Andres said, "This is pagan talk. We should not be listening to this."

"Don't listen to it, then," Ulf said.

"What he means is that we should not be saying it," Bjarni said.

"That's the law," Andres said.

"My mother," Ulf said, "should never have started listening to priests. Well, she did not womanize me. I still know what a man does."

"I don't see we are such heroes," Jon said. "We took Papa's ship away just before the herring fishing. We left him and Stepmother with no one to cut wood or haul water—"

"Yes," Andres said. "They can't do all the work by themselves."

Bjarni rubbed his thumb over the runes he had made in the wood of the oar-blade. He looked up at the sun. He had marked Jon and Andres talking earnestly together earlier in the day. The other men in the ship were watching them covertly.

"They don't have to feed us all, either," Ulf said. "*Swan* was battered on a rock last year, and we all fished from one of Eirik Arnarson's boats. Papa can do that again."

"It isn't fair," Jon said.

"Bah. Which of us has he not struck unfairly?"

"He has never struck me," Kristjan said.

"Because if he did your mother would hit him over the head with the axe," Ulf said.

Jon laughed.

"Or a fire-iron," Kristjan said. He gave Bjarni a dagger of a look.

"I think we should go back," Andres said. "We can take Bjarni to this Sigmund—"

"Sigurd," Bjarni said.

"There, and we can go back to Iceland."

"Missing two oars," Ulf said. "Because I am not going back."

"I think we ought to go home now," Andres said. "All of us."

"We would look like fools!"

"It's the right thing to do."

Jon said, "He can't thrash us all, not all at once."

"Bjarni," Andres said. "What do you think?"

Bjarni had finished cutting the charm into the oar. He slid the long shaft down under the bench and stowed it along the keel with his foot.

"I am going to the Hebrides," he said. "There are four-teen other men in this ship besides you. I've been lucky so far. Most of them will stay with me. You won't find enough men to sail *Swan*." He nodded to Andres and Jon. "If you want to go back to Hrafnfell, I will see that you get home again."

Their faces settled, but they did not argue. Kristjan was looking away, over the rail of the ship. Bjarni folded his arms over his chest. To Ulf, he said, "Do you remember the story about Jarl Hakon and the Jomsvikings?"

His brother grinned and struck his palms together. "Tell me."

"We should not listen," Andres said.

"Just a little," Jon said. "A little will do no hurt."

THAT NIGHT was the darkest since they had left Iceland. They were farther south than Bjarni had ever been before. Most of the men slept. In the bow two played chess under a little torch. Bjarni shielded his eyes from the light. He sat in the stern with his head tipped back to watch the stars. He thought of Hiyke, of how he had hidden his lust from her for so long, and then at the very end had let it burn her.

He thought of the runes on the oar-blade:

Here I sit threshing Amleth's corn
While the lazy man
Washes his hair in the mill-pond

The work of Hrafnfell had shaped every day of his past. Now his life was featureless as the open ocean. It daunted him; yet he yearned toward it, wondering. He put his arms behind his head and lay back in the stern of the ship. Overhead the stars turned in their wheel.

FOR SEVERAL DAYS THEY SAILED down past a string of islands, keeping to windward. As they passed, a long plume of smoke rose from the crest of one island. To the south more smoke appeared. Bjarni stood in the stern to watch. The chart put Sigurd Gormsson's stronghold somewhere in the clutter of islands whose green tops jutted up along the southern horizon. The sailing there was difficult; the chart was muddled. But he thought the smoke would bring him a pilot.

All the rest of the day, as they sailed south along the

island chain, columns of smoke signaled their passage on ahead of them. In the late afternoon, a big longship rowed out of the south. Bjarni put the steerboard over.

The longship flew over the sea. She was three times the length of *Swan*, and her black oars swept the sea like wings.

"Hail, ship!"

Bjarni made a horn of his hands. "This is *Swan*," he shouted, "and I am Bjarni Hoskuldsson, from Iceland— I look for Sigurd Gormsson."

The great longship drew even with them. All along *Swan*, the Icelanders sighed and gaped at the stranger.

"Hoskuld's son?" called a man on the big ship. He was dressed all in black, but his long hair and his beard were grey, like fox fur. "Would that be Hoskuld the Ganger?"

"Yes," Bjarni answered. "He says that you and he were friends in the old days."

Now only a few ells separated the ships. The man in black looked quizzical. "How do you know who I am?"

"You knew Hoskuld. Aren't you Sigurd Gormsson? He sent me here to join you."

Sigurd's lips stretched in an unpleasant smile. "Did he, now? Just you, or the whole kennel there?"

"They go with me. And the ship."

"The ship!" Sigurd laughed, and set his ship's crew to laughing. "She looks like a dirty little fishing boat to me. Likely she stinks of fish."

Ulf started up; Bjarni put his foot on his brother's

shoulder and pushed him down again. He said, across the water, "She's a trim little ship, she will sail closer to the wind than that hulk of yours."

Sigurd laughed again, and his crew laughed. "Well, come inshore and let me measure you. I have some need of men, I may take you in."

The Icelanders rowed *Swan* after the longship toward a hump-backed island whose green slopes ran down to meet the water. On the shore there were buildings, some hardly more than sties, but others were great halls with carved wooden doors, and windows in the thatched roofs. Sigurd's sleek longship led the Icelanders around the northern end of the island, and a cove opened up before them. In the quiet water six or eight ships rocked at their anchors; two others were drawn up on the beach.

Sigurd bade them anchor in the cove. The men on *Swan* gawked at the island and the other ships, shouting and pointing their fingers. Bjarni and his brothers rowed the little boat in to the shore.

A hall dominated the slope over the cove. To one side of it was a big Christian temple with a cross on the gable, and many other smaller buildings were scattered around on the green grass. Boardwalks, lifted up above the ground on piles, connected the doors.

Sigurd met the Hoskuldssons on the shore, three or four other men waiting at his beck nearby. When Bjarni came up the beach toward him, Sigurd squared his shoulders and put his hands on his belt.

"Yes, you are Hoskuld's son, you are the image of him."

They shook hands. Sigurd led him to the high side of

the beach, where the boardwalk began, and they climbed the rattling wooden planks toward the hall. Bjarni walked beside Sigurd, with his brothers following after. Sigurd pointed to the other buildings scattered around the meadow on either side of the boardwalk.

"I have my own forge, you see. My own mill. My own church. I am no pirate; here, my men have wives and children, some even farm. It is the Bishop who is the pirate—him I mean to fight."

Ahead of them two dark-haired women waited on the threshold of the hall. Sigurd nodded to them. "These are my wives."

Besides two wives he had children ranging from grown sons to babies. Bjarni saw that Ulf's eyes fell on one of the older daughters.

"So you wish to enter my service," Sigurd said. He took Bjarni into the hall and up to the High Seat before the hearth. "Can you fight? You don't carry any weapons. I suppose you want me to arm you as well."

"I am not asking to serve you." Bjarni sat down on the bench on Sigurd's right. He looked around him at the hall, which was twice as large as Hrafnfell's, and so wide there were three rows of wooden pillars to hold up the roofbeams. The broad benches down the sides of the room were covered with hides and blankets; men slept there. He turned to Sigurd again.

"I don't want to serve anybody, now that I am free of my father. I will help you, if we can come to an agreement. I'm a good sailor, and I can fight."

"You didn't listen to me, outside. I am no pirate. I rule

here. We have order here. You serve me, or you don't stay here."

Bjarni raised his shoulders in a shrug. Rather than lift up his eyes to Sigurd in the High Seat, he studied the hall, and the people going in and out; Ulf had already sat down with Sigurd's blond daughter on the far side of the hearth.

"I don't serve anybody," Bjarni said. "I will go on, if you want it so. How long has it been since you saw Iceland?"

"I am no Icelander."

"I am."

Sigurd grunted in his throat. A serving man brought each of them a cup. Bjarni's was of wood but Sigurd's cup was of red-gold.

"I also have my own brewhouse," he said.

Bjarni tasted the beer. "This is very good." He drank it all, and the servant brought him more.

"Hoskuld the Walker," Sigurd said. "I recall something else about Hoskuld, which is that he ate of the horse. Are you a Christian?"

"Everyone is Christian in Iceland. We are all baptized."

"By the law, yes. In the heart is another matter. Everyone knows that. Do you sacrifice to Christ?"

"No, I am Thor's man."

Sigurd canted forward over the table, so that Bjarni had to look at him. He said, "You shall have to be a Christian to serve me. I will not let the Bishop claim I am harboring pagans."

"I can see that we don't agree on anything," Bjarni said. "I keep the law, but I have no interest in Christ, or any hanged god, for that matter."

"Yes, you are Hoskuld's son. He might have been one of my chief men, but instead he went back to drying fish and milking goats and a straw death in Iceland."

Bjarni drank a third cup of the thick foamy beer. He and Sigurd spoke of the voyage from Iceland. All the while, men came in and went out of the hall. They were richly dressed, and all of them carried some weapon, most of them more than one.

"Hoskuld was a good fighter," Sigurd said. "Something might be made of you, although you seem milder than he. Stay on awhile, I will convince you that your fortunes lie with me."

"I will stay," Bjarni said, "until you convince me otherwise."

At that Sigurd laughed again.

The men of *Swan* brought their sea-chests into a small sleeping booth near the water and made their beds there. When the sun set, they went to the hall.

Now it was thick with men. Two big casks of beer were open by the door, and the men came and dunked their drinking cups and strode off, their sleeves dripping. At the table Sigurd was talking to some other men, and there were people bent over chess-games. Along the side of the hearth a boy cranked a roast on the spit.

Sigurd's fair daughter came to them. Smiling, she took them through the crowd to a bench where they might sit, and she and another girl brought them bread and cheese to eat. Ulf tried to speak to her; he caught at her skirt, but she whisked it away, laughing at him. She was back in a moment and sat down beside him.

Andres and Jon sat crouched together on the bench. "This is a thieves' den," Andres said, between his teeth. "Keep your hand on your pennies."

Bjarni wondered if Andres had ever owned a penny. Most of the Icelanders had already drifted away through Sigurd's men toward the beer kegs. Kristjan stood near a wooden pillar, his dark eyes moving. His mother's eyes were blue. Bjarni stirred; he went away from his brothers, around the hearth.

Being taller than most of the men he could see what went on. He strolled around the hall, watching Sigurd's men talking and gaming. The blond girl had given him a cup; he filled it with beer. Presently he found an empty place on a bench before the hearth and sat down. He meant not to think of Hiyke, but he did.

"That is my place," a loud voice said.

Beside him was a burly man with blue and red feathers in his beard. All the men nearby quieted, turning to watch. Sigurd was watching, his elbows braced on the table.

"That is my place," the feathered man said again, and kicked at Bjarni's leg.

Bjarni moved his leg out of the way. "Is that so," he said. "Then you may have it when I get up."

"I said it is my place!"

The feathered man lunged at him. Bjarni jumped to

his feet and drove his fist into the man's broad belly. A yell went up from the other men watching. The burly man swung his arm roundabout at Bjarni's head, and Bjarni hit him again just below the ribs. The man fell.

Surprised, Bjarni backed away; he had not expected to win so easily. At the High Seat, Sigurd was standing, his hand raised. All the men in the hall waited for his words. Sigurd spread his lips in his ugly smile.

"Here is Lyr fallen, does he have no friends to help him?"

"I'm Lyr's friend," a voice bawled, from the other side of the hearth, and a red-haired man strode through the crowd toward Bjarni.

Bjarni stepped backward, away from Lyr, and turned to put his back to the hearth. He glanced once at Sigurd, beaming in his place at the High Seat. The red-headed man charged, his arms milling.

Bjarni knocked his first blows out of the way; the red-headed man tripped him, and they fell. The red-headed man sank his teeth into Bjarni's shoulder. Bjarni hit him twice in the head. His hand turned numb but the red-head, dazed, opened his jaws, and Bjarni threw him off. He lurched up onto his knees.

Already another man was coming at him from the crowd. Behind the solid wall of men, Ulf shouted. Bjarni called, "Stay back!" He jumped to his feet to meet the man coming toward him.

That was a small man, but tough and fast, who hit him twice before Bjarni knocked him into the mob. Then a bald man charged him too exuberantly, and Bjarni stepped off at the right moment and tripped him into the fire. Blood was running down Bjarni's cheek from a cut in his eyebrow; he sobbed for breath. Another man was circling toward him, crouched like a wrestler.

Bjarni moved away from him, trying to gain his breath. The fire heated his back. He could not escape from this. It was Sigurd who was directing it. He strode into the wrestler, wishing it were Sigurd, and they exchanged some blows and Sigurd's man fell.

The yelling of the mob rang in his ears. He pawed at the cut over his eye and the blood got into the eye and half-blinded him. Another man was edging toward him, wary, his arms up over his face.

"I hope you will not hold this against me," Bjarni said. He swung at the man's head and missed.

The man dodged to the left. He grinned, showing gapped teeth. "I will forgive hundreds of those," he said.

"Then you won't mind this one." Bjarni wheeled his right arm again at the man's jaw.

Sigurd's man dodged to the left again, and Bjarni met him with his left fist, straight in the pit of his gut. The man sat down hard, his eyes filming over. Already his replacement was elbowing out of the crowd.

Bjarni swayed on his feet; his fists hurt, and his eye was full of blood. He knew he would go down soon. He hated Sigurd for this; he would never join Sigurd now. The next man came at him all in a rush, shouting, and butted him in the stomach, and Bjarni got him by the belt and threw him back against the hearth.

He had lost count. His breath sawed in and out of his throat. The man facing him now was as tall as he was, almost as brawny, and fresh as new milk. They stood foot to foot pounding each other on the chest and shoulders. Bjarni slipped and went to one knee and a fist smashed into the side of his head. His eyes lost their power to see. He found himself on his feet again, his arms pumping. Through a red mist he saw the other big man go down.

Still there was another. He could scarcely lift his arms. He fell again and staggered up and fell without a hand laid on him. The cheers of Sigurd's men resounded over him. He could not move. A black sleep took him.

WHEN HE CAME BACK to himself he was lying on a bench in the sleeping booth where his crew was quartered. The morning sun shone in the window. Ulf and his brothers were sitting around him. Ulf brought him a bucket of water to wash in.

"Why didn't you lie down when you saw what the game was?"

Bjarni snarled at him. His lip and eye were swollen and when he moved, his muscles ached. He pushed Jon and Andres away from him and bent over the bucket of water.

"We tried to help you," Jon said. "Why are you angry with us?

"Get out of here," Bjarni said. It hurt to talk. He dipped his hands into the cold water.

"You sound like Papa," Andres said. He and Jon left the booth.

Bjarni washed his face and his filthy hands, scabbed with dirt and blood. Ulf sat watching him in silence. Bjarni could not look at him; the memory of his humiliation burned in him. There was no one else in the booth. He was ashamed to go out, ashamed to see the men who had beaten him, and he prolonged the washing. The door at the other end of the booth opened.

"Cover yourselves," a woman called.

Bjarni straightened; Ulf slid off the bench to his feet. "Gudrun," he called.

Sigurd's blond daughter came down the booth toward them, a basket under her arm. She passed through the slice of daylight under the window and the light shone over her wheaten hair and creamy skin.

"I have brought you some food," she said, and set the basket down.

"Stay," Ulf said. He caught hold of her hand.

"I must go," she said.

But she sat down willingly enough beside Ulf on the bench. She smiled at Bjarni and said, "You are quite a fighting man. My father is much pleased with you."

Bjarni wiped his face on a towel. Ulf was holding the girl's hand on his knee and looking into her face, and she put her hand on his chest and pushed him.

"No, go away, you are very familiar. I'm not even supposed to come in here." She pushed him again, smiling at him.

"Just a little while," Ulf said. He took cheese and meat from the basket. "Share this with us."

"I am going," Bjarni said. He went down the sleeping booth toward the door. The roofbeams crossed just over his head, trailing cobwebs, and he beat them down with his hands. At the door he glanced back to see Ulf and Gudrun sitting together in the half-dark, laughing. Ulf fed her a piece of a bun.

"I must go," she said, and giggled, and made no attempt to rise. Bjarni went out of the booth.

Swan was moored in among the longships. Her broad beam and chopped prow made her loutish by comparison. Bjarni collected some of his crew and they refitted her, mending rigging and filling her watercasks. No one said anything about the fight. Carefully no one looked at Bjarni's bruises. His hands bothered him. In the stern he came on the oar with the runes on it. He touched the rune called the Hammer, where it occurred in several words, and swore that he would repay Sigurd. After that his mood lightened. He went back to the shore.

Kristjan was standing there on the beach. When Bjarni pulled the ship's boat up onto the cobbles Hiyke's son called to him.

"Lord Sigurd wants to see you in the hall."

Bjarni made the boat's painter fast to a stump. "Why were you talking to him?"

Kristjan sidled away down the beach. "He asked me a few questions." He turned his back to Bjarni and went off.

Bjarni found Sigurd in the hall, eating, with a servant behind him to hold his napkin. When Bjarni came into the hall Sigurd put down the meat bone in his hands. He looked Bjarni over well before he spoke. Bjarni was willing to wait for his revenge; he could be civil now, and he let Sigurd look.

"I understand you are stocking your ship," the older man said. "Have we frightened you away?"

"I don't mind a little fighting," Bjarni said. He stood across the table from Sigurd. "I don't like that you questioned my stepbrother."

Sigurd picked the bone from the table and set his teeth to it again. "He is not a talkative child."

"We are all together, we Icelanders," Bjarni said. "You talk to us all when you talk to me."

"Hoskuld hates you. Now, why would he send me a son he hates? It sounds to me as if he wants you done away with."

"I don't know about that," Bjarni said. "Neither does Kristjan."

Sigurd snapped his fingers and the servant brought him the napkin so that the lord could wipe his greasy beard. He drank from his gold cup. Voices sounded at the far end of the hall. Footsteps ground on the floor. Sigurd struck the table with his palm.

"You are an innocent," he said to Bjarni. "No one lives the way you want to live. In this world, everyone has his master; everyone has his underlings. I can protect you from your father. Serve me, fight for me, obey me, and I will make you rich. But you must take Christ."

"My god is Asa-Thor," Bjarni said.

"Your stepbrother says that all save you are Christian."

"All save me and Ulf. His mother turned to the white altars when he was weaned. What about this Bishop you are warring with? Is he not a Christian? I thought you loved one another, you Christians."

"The Bishop is a false priest who claims lands where I alone am lord," Sigurd said. "But you do not see the advantages in taking Christ. Your god-goat gives you nothing. I need only repent at the proper moment, and Christ will give me life eternal."

"Do you have to die first? Then I don't see that he gives you very much."

Sigurd thrust his empty cup at the servant, who took it at a run down the table. The lord thrust his grey head forward toward Bjarni. The shredded gold flashed on his sleeves and collar. When he spoke he pushed each word at Bjarni with a bobbing of his head.

"Your goat-god, your dirty-handed farmer-god, did he save you from the beating last night? Can he save you from death?"

"Every man comes to die," Bjarni said. "It is the price of life. There is no choice in it, save to meet it well."

"That is the weakness in the old way, do you not see? If there is no choice, a man is worthless, the slave of Fate. Christ has freed us from that."

"Free. You have no claim on that word. You Christians are ever telling folk how to act."

"A man can sin," Sigurd said.

"You leave me unconvinced."

"Because you will not bend your mind," Sigurd said. He tossed the picked bone under the table. "We shall argue again—I enjoy this. In time you will agree. Now take leave of me, I must talk to these other men."

He rose from the High Seat and walked off along the table, his hand stretched out to a small troop of new-comers. Bjarni turned slowly away from the table.

Sigurd's men were coming in and out of the hall. Some stood idly talking by the door, and some were drinking. Bjarni had seen no one here do any work, except the servants. The belts of the men were stuffed with knives and swords and hatchets. On their arms they wore heavy bracelets of gold, and there were gold rings in their ears and on their fingers. Bjarni was a misfit here, poorer than the servants. His gaze caught on a man sitting on the bench by the fire.

It was Lyr, the burly man with the feathers in his beard, who had started the fight. Bjarni went around the hearth to him.

"Get up," he said.

The feathered man raised his startled face. He looked to right and left; there was room on the bench.

"Get up," Bjarni said again.

Reluctantly the burly man stood. He watched uncer-tainly as Bjarni took his place on the bench. After a moment he slunk away down the hall.

.   .   .

Two MORE LONGSHIPS rowed into the cove between then and nightfall. In the crowded anchorage, Bjarni took the ship's small boat again and again around *Swan,* directing his brothers inside the ship to move the ballast here and there, so that *Swan* rode better in the water.

"When shall we sail?" Andres said.

He sat in the stern of the boat; Bjarni and Jon were rowing back to the beach.

"Do you have someplace to go?" Bjarni asked.

"Anywhere but here," Andres said, intensely. "This is a wicked place."

"He's right," Jon said, behind Bjarni at the bow oars. "Let's go back to Iceland. These people are sinners."

Bjarni trailed his oars to turn the boat. The little waves of the surf lifted her sideways up onto the gravelly beach. "I have been beaten worse in Iceland. Hop out."

His half brothers sprang out of the boat, and he waited for another wave to carry him higher on the shore and got out onto the land. They dragged the boat out of the surf. Jon walked on his left, Andres on his right, and they flung arguments at him, none convincing. They were both a head shorter than he was. Their fair faces, broad and stub-nosed, reminded him of Hoskuld. He let them argue and said nothing.

They went into the little booth where *Swan*'s crew slept. The men from the two new longships were staying there as well and the place was crowded. Ulf sat on the wooden bench where he slept; he smiled, and in his hands held a piece of fine linen.

"What is that?" Jon said.

Ulf held it out to him. "Smell of it."

Bjarni took a bucket out the door and filled it from the rainbarrel under the eave. When he came in again, Jon was holding the linen at arm's length. It was a piece of a woman's underclothing, the top piece. Jon threw it down.

"You will get us all in trouble," Andres hissed, and glanced around them at the other men scattered through the dark room.

Bjarni set the bucket on the bench, stripped off his shirt, and washed himself. Ulf was grinning. He took the linen in his hands and sniffed it and laid it against his cheek.

"I notice there's only one piece," Bjarni said. He splashed cold water on his arms.

"If she lets me in the loft," Ulf said, "she'll let me into the kitchen."

Bjarni stooped over the bucket and scooped water onto his face. He scrubbed himself and dried himself and combed his hair and his beard. He was of a mind to stay here until he heard more about the Bishop and the war; but Ulf and Gudrun were adding to the risks of that. He took a clean shirt out of his sea-chest and put it on.

"I am going to the hall," he said. "Are you coming?"

Jon and Andres rounded on him, their eyes wide, and spoke at once. "You are mad. Do you like being beaten?" Andres said, "They are all sinners."

Bjarni shrugged. He left the sleeping booth. The sun had set. Streaks of red and orange lay across the sky; in the east, the night had come. A cold wind touched his cheek. The boardwalk resounded under the feet of the streams of men on their way to the hall. The little waves of the cove lapped on the shore. The water was dark as death. The longships slapped and creaked at their moorings. His eyes fastened on a high coiled prow, black against the ruddy sky. The beauty stirred his heart. All his life he had heard of such ships, of the glory of the men who sailed them. Maybe in those earlier days the men had been different. He saw nothing glorious in Sigurd's men, falling as soon as he hit them so that another could take the fight. He went up the boardwalk toward the crowded hall.

He ate; he drank beer; he found someone to play chess with him. While he was studying a difficult position Sigurd called him to the High Seat.

"Tell your brother to leave off courting my daughter," Sigurd said.

The table's breadth was between them, littered with food and cups. Bjarni set his hand on it. He said, "I don't see that she objects."

"I object," Sigurd said. He waggled his finger at Bjarni. "You do something about it. Then come back. I have some work for you and your ship."

Bjarni went down the hall. The door was open and he stepped past the men coming through it, out to the evening air. A mist was rising out of the damp grass. Off to his left, halfway down the boardwalk to the beach, was the Christian temple, and Ulf and Gudrun were sitting on the porch together. Bjarni went down to them.

"Come over here a moment," he said to Ulf.

They went a few yards down the boardwalk. Bjarni said, "Her father just spoke to me about you and this girl."

"Oh? Is he talking about a dowry?"

"No, he wants me to tell you to leave her alone."

Ulf grunted. He put his hands on his hips. "Damn him. No. Tell him I have not trifled with her. Tell him—" His face worked. "Tell him I will marry her."

"He also has some work for *Swan*. After I have told you to leave his daughter alone." Bjarni turned his eyes down the dark slope. The mist blurred the shapes of the longships on the water.

"He is ready to attack the Bishop," Ulf said. "Maybe he will use us as a scout." He glanced to either side. A file of men trampled past them, dividing to go by them on the plank walk. Under his breath, Ulf said, "I can see Gudrun in secret."

"I am not telling you to leave her," Bjarni said. "I do not take his orders. Go tell our crew to load their chests into the ship."

Ulf grinned at him. "You are a very stubborn man."

"We will be in some trouble before long," Bjarni said. He went back to the hall.

After an hour or so had passed Sigurd called to him again. He went up before the High Seat.

"Is your ship ready to sail?" Sigurd said. "You will take one of my pilots here with you and sail south with a message for the Bishop."

"You are going too fast," Bjarni said. "We have not agreed yet on the terms of our partnership."

"Partnership! Listen, Bjarni Hoskuldsson. This is the agreement. You will do as I say, and take the share everyone takes, and you will do it happily because better men than you are doing it."

"I don't agree to that," Bjarni said.

"I don't care if you do or not," Sigurd said. His neck swelled. He spoke in volleys of words. "That is my decision. You will kneel down at Mass tomorrow with the rest of us, or I will put you in stocks on the beach."

Bjarni went out of the hall. Ulf was outside on the boardwalk. He fell into step beside Bjarni. They walked down the rackety boardwalk toward the beach.

"Are we leaving?" Ulf said.

"Yes. Let's hurry before he decides to take the ship."

"Gudrun." Ulf stopped and looked back. Bjarni caught his arm.

"Hurry."

Jon stood on the threshold of the sleeping booth; he blinked at them as if he had just wakened. He said, "What is the matter?" Bjarni stopped at the edge of the beach. The other men from *Swan* were gathering below them on the gravel. On the hillside above them, in the mist, each of the hall lights wore a ring.

"I don't want to leave Gudrun," Ulf said, beside Bjarni.

"I haven't time to argue with you." Bjarni pushed his younger brothers ahead of him. Ulf hung back, his tongue busy.

"We can take her with us. I know she will go."

"Later."

"Just let me talk to her."

"Later."

They reached the edge of the water. The boat was already at the ship; Kristjan and another man were unloading the sea-chests from it. Bjarni and the others waded out to *Swan*.

"Ulf," Bjarni said. "Go into the bow and guide us. Put out the oars."

On the hillside near the hall someone shouted.

They rowed *Swan* out of the anchorage. Sigurd did not chase them. Bjarni took *Swan* on her legs out to sea and turned her bow to the wind. The other men lay down in the hold to sleep. Bjarni and his brothers sat in the bow.

"What did you do?" Kristjan said. "You ruined our chances with them. It was his fault, wasn't it?" He pointed to Ulf.

"Now we can all go back to Hrafnfell," Jon said.

"Maybe," Bjarni said. "We have nothing to eat and we need line and canvas. Tomorrow I want to raid Sigurd for supplies."

Ulf opened the lid of his sea-chest and took out a bearskin. In a low voice, he said, "If we can steal food, we can steal Gudrun."

"Why don't you forget her?" Bjarni said. "You hardly know her."

Ulf struck his shoulder. "Because I love her. Anyway, this will make it a real raid. We can't go home with nothing, we will be shamed."

Jon said, "But—" and Andres elbowed him in the ribs.
"Be quiet. With a woman aboard we will have to go
back to Iceland."

"Sigurd has a hundred men," Kristjan said. "What you
are talking about is impossible. We can fish for food."

Bjarni said, "There is a way to do it." To Ulf, he said,
"Tomorrow they are sacrificing in their temple."

Jon shot up onto his feet. The ship teetered under him.
"You can't fight in a church."

"They won't take weapons into a church," Bjarni said.

"Isn't Sigurd leaving soon to fight against the Bishop?"
Kristjan said. He looked from Bjarni to Ulf. "Wait until
he goes, and we can take everything we want."

Ulf said, "You churlish Irish sneak-thief."

Andres said, "Well, really, either way, it's stealing."

Bjarni stood and left them there to argue. He went back
to the stern and fell asleep.

IN THE MORNING Sigurd's men went to the church, and
Bjarni took *Swan* back into the cove. The Icelanders broke
into the storerooms above the beach and took meat and
cheeses and grain. Ulf and Bjarni went up the grassy
slope toward the Christian temple. Ulf was looking around
them at the other ships in the cove.

"There are twice as many ships here as there were last
night," he said.

"Just move fast," Bjarni said. "It doesn't matter how
many there are if they can't catch us."

"What happens if we are caught?" Ulf said. They climbed the walk toward the temple.

"That depends on you," Bjarni said. "I promise you that if Sigurd takes you he will take me also."

He looked over his shoulder. His crew was scrambling up over *Swan*'s rails and settling at their places. From the bow, Jon waved to him.

"They are ready. Let's go."

They went into the church through the front door. The altar was at the other end of the building and the Christians were kneeling, so that their backs were to the door. Ulf and Bjarni went in among them. Gudrun knelt in the first row; three or four people were between her and Sigurd. No one noticed the Hoskuldssons until Ulf reached her side and pulled her to her feet.

A roar went up from the Christian men. Ulf hoisted the girl over his shoulder and ran down the room toward the door. Sigurd bellowed. His men swarmed after Ulf.

Bjarni went out the door. He let his brother through and slammed the door shut. The bar was tilted against the wall; he seized it and pressed it over the double door to hold it shut. Before he could fit the long bar into the iron brackets over the door, Sigurd and his men reached the other side.

Their first rush nearly threw the doors open. He strained against them. The doors bulged and he saw, through the gap into the church, Sigurd's face red as fire. Bjarni shoved with all his strength on the bar and forced the doors shut. The bar slipped into the brackets. He wheeled to run.

A shout sounded on the other side of the building. Someone had gotten out the side window. Bjarni raced down the boardwalk; where it swerved off his course he jumped down to the marshy grass and ran for *Swan*. Right behind him came the man who had climbed out the window. Ulf had reached the water and was splashing out to the ship. Gudrun waded beside him, her hand in his.

With a splintering crash the church door gave way and spilled Sigurd and his men out after Bjarni. He glanced over his shoulder. The man behind was almost within reach of him.

Swan rocked from side to side. Ulf was climbing inboard. Bjarni drove himself faster. The men in *Swan* were not waiting for him. Their oars ran out. They leaned into the first stroke. A body struck him from behind, just above the knees, and he fell hard onto the cobbles of the beach.

SIGURD'S MEN BOUND HIM and threw him into a storeroom. There he lay for hours, trussed up so tight his fingers went to sleep.

Eventually Sigurd came into the storeroom. He said, "That was an unfriendly thing to do."

"I'm sorry to offend your hospitality," Bjarni said. He was lying on his face. By twisting his head he could look up at Sigurd, but he had no wish to see him; he lay still, with Sigurd's boots before his eyes.

"You know, your brothers are not coming back for

you," Sigurd said. "We chased them for above three hours, and they went due west, straight for the north-running sea." Sigurd squatted down to peer into Bjarni's face. "I only wish I had your sneaking brother Ulf as well as you. I don't care so much for my daughter, and neither will he when he knows her better, but I want to repay him for robbing me in my own church."

"You don't need Ulf for that," Bjarni said. "That was my idea."

"Was it," Sigurd said. "Then I will have my revenge after all."

He walked up and down the storeroom, through the fringes of dried fish that dangled from the beams. Bjarni worked the ropes that bound his wrists. His brothers would return for him; they were only putting Sigurd off. Sigurd came back and sank down on his hams before him.

"My old friend Hoskuld was right about you, and right to send you here. You will be useless to anyone until you are broken. And I am the man to do it."

He went out of the storeroom. When he came back he had a smith with him, and a length of chain.

During the day Bjarni was chained to the mill, and he ground the corn. At night he was chained to an anvil in the forge. The first night, he tried with all his strength to move the anvil, but it would not yield.

Sigurd loaded his men into their longships and sailed away to fight the Bishop. Ulf and *Swan* did not come back.

Every day Bjarni walked around the mill turning the millstone. Every night he tried to move the anvil. For seven days his strength was nothing to the weight of the anvil, but on the eighth night, when he heaved against it, he felt it move.

When he thought of his brothers, he clenched his fists around the spoke of the millstone; he set his shoulders and ground his anger with the oats and rye. He thought much of Hiyke, in Hrafnfell, his father's wife.

She was not really Hoskuld's wife. She had come to live with them four years before. Hoskuld's second wife had been long dead; at Hrafnfell they were used to being bachelors, although Bjarni knew that his father was blanket-wise with a woman beyond the mountains. Then one spring she came across the pass to Hrafnfell, leading her black-haired boy by the hand. In the summer, she miscarried. She and Hoskuld never married.

As he trudged behind the spoke of the millstone, he tried to make poems of her. He made one for his father.

> *Odinn slew*
> *The son of Loki*
> *Made ropes of his guts*
> *To bind his father*
> *Would you were Loki*
> *I would lust for death*

He had no words for Hiyke.

On the fifteenth night, he moved the anvil five feet across the forge to the hearth.

He laid the chain in the coals and pumped the bellows. When the links began to glow, he stretched them across the anvil. He knew some charms for smiths and said them, although he could not hammer the links for fear of bringing down the Christians; he wrapped his hands around the cooler part of the chain and pulled, heated the links and pulled them until the stretching iron broke.

Dawn was coming. He found a knife and an axe in the forge and took them down to the shore. The cove was deserted. It looked much wider with the longships gone. Three or four smaller boats were drawn up on the beach.

He found oars in one, sails in another, and put the oars into the boat with the sails. All the while he considered what he might do to avenge himself on Sigurd. He could fire some of the buildings, but that would waken the people in the place just as he was trying to steal away. He would have to wait for his revenge. Bjarni filled a bucket with fresh water from the rainbarrel and stowed it into the boat. In the silent dawn he rowed out of the cove.

When he left the lee of the island, the wind freshened, and he stepped the mast and raised the sail. The boat flew before the wind. The islands shrank in the distance and slid below the horizon. The rigging sang like harps. The rudder worked in his hands. Until well into the day he let the boat go where the wind blew.

His wrists were still locked up to the chain. He wrapped the dangling lengths of the chain around his arms and tied them to keep them out of his way. In a locker under the stern thwart there were line and hooks of fishbone. He stabbed his finger with the hook to bloody it and cast the line out behind his boat.

The wind was out of the north. Dark cloudbanks lay along the horizon. He put the boat on a broad reach, running to the east. In the afternoon he caught two stockfish. While he was boning them with his knife the humps of a mountainous island rose out of the sea to the east. He took the sail down and ran out the oars.

He spent the night on the shore. In the morning the wind was foul and he rowed the boat northward. Islands dotted the water. His fishing line snagged on hidden rocks. He kept watch for reefs. The wind was so cold he could not sleep all that night; he rowed to keep warm. In the sunlit morning he landed on a little island and slept.

Clouds covered the sun. The wind veered around to the southwest. Bjarni raised his sail. The boat ran north over rising waves. The water chuckled past the rudder. Rain began to fall. Bjarni was reluctant to give up the fair wind; he did not run into the shelter of an island.

The wind rose. The boat began to buck and shy along the waves. Water spilled over the railings. He brought in the sail. Gradually the dark was settling over him. There were islands to his left, but the battering waves burst in plumes of spray along their shores. If he landed he would lose the boat. The storm roared around him. He flung the sail over to act as a sea-anchor. He bailed with the bucket, his knees wedged against the thwarts to keep him with the boat. The boat sounded and swooped over the wild sea. His hands were numb and his mouth was full of salt. With the coming of daylight, the storm passed.

He lay exhausted in the boat with his head on the gun-

wale rail. In fitful sleep he dreamt of giants and of burning in the wolf-sister's hall.

When he woke the boat was floating on the open sea.
The sun rolled through clouds. The mast was gone, lost
overboard in the storm. His knife was gone, and the bucket
and the fishing line. The wind was blowing out of the
north again. He put out the oars and poled the boat north.

He was thirsty and hungry and his back hurt. Darkness
fell; the sky was starless. He shivered all night. In the
morning he licked the dew from the iron links of the
chain around his wrists.

There were clouds mounded up in the sky to the east.
He thought there might be land under them, and he put
his back into the oars. All that day he rowed under the
pale sun. His tongue swelled with thirst. When he looked
over his shoulder to see where he was going, his gaze met
only the heaving sea.

Night closed over him. He rowed on in the dark. He
had ceased to think or feel anything. He dragged the oars
through the water and raised them and dipped them back
into the sea again. He forgot to look behind him. The
first he knew that he had reached land was the grating
of the keel on the pebbly shore.

He climbed out of the boat into knee-deep water. The
air was bitter with woodsmoke. A cliff leaned out over
the beach. The beach ended in rocks. The cliff curved
away into the darkness, and in the distance, a fire burned.

He looped the chain over his shoulders and walked
along the foot of the cliff toward the light. When the

beach gave out he walked in the sea. His eyes were fixed on the fire.

"Halt."

There was someone on the cliff above him, and he stopped walking, to his waist in the surf. The fire was only twenty feet away.

"Who is there?"

The men around the fire stood and backed away from the light. The man on the cliff was shouting at him again.

"Put up your hands, and stand where you are."

He lifted his hands over his head to show he was harmless and walked forward up the shore toward the fire. His tongue was too thick for speech. One of the men gathered behind the fire came to meet him and stood in front of him, at the edge of the waves.

This was an old man. A white beard covered his chest. He had a knife for boning fish in his hand. Bjarni stopped, still in the icy water.

"Whose chains are those, before you use our fire?"

Bjarni croaked, "Sigurd Gormsson's."

"Come." The fisherman sheathed his knife and led him to the fire.

They gave him water and covered him with blankets. He shed his wet clothes. The white-bearded man sat down beside him in the firelight.

"What business did you have with Sigurd Clench-Fist?"

"That's a long story," Bjarni said.

"Eat first," the fisherman said.

They gave him bread and baked fish. The bread was

gritty and studded with bits of chaff. While he ate he told them what had happened between him and Sigurd Gormsson. The other fishermen sat there listening.

"Everything good, Sigurd steals," the white-bearded man said. "That is how we value goods around here—'not worth Sigurd's stealing.' What is your name?"

"Bjarni Hoskuldsson."

"Barney. That fits you, you are as big as a bear. You eat like a bear, too."

Bjarni put down what was left of the loaf. "I will work. I don't beg."

The fisherman's head nodded.

"What island is this?" Bjarni asked.

"This island has no name—we have only pulled in here to wait out the storm. We live on the mainland, in Fenby. Jarl Robert is our lord, and our king is William the Red." The fisherman was looking Bjarni over closely. He saw the amulet Bjarni wore around his neck. "That is a strange cross. Where do you live?"

"Iceland," Bjarni said. The amulet was in the shape of Thor's Hammer; it looked somewhat like a cross. "I have heard of a king named Rufus. Is that the same man as William the Red?"

"Yes. Red William. Praise God there is only one." The fisherman signed himself in the Christian way, and the others did also. "You must be tired. We will let you rest." He went off to the other side of the fire. The other fishermen followed, talking to each other of Bjarni.

In the morning when the sun shone again, the six fishermen put off in their boat and sailed across a narrow sound toward the mainland. Their boat was clumsy and over-loaded with fish. Bjarni helped them with the sail. The boat wallowed in toward the low hills of the mainland.

Bjarni watched the shore. That was England, half across the world from Iland. He had heard more of England in stories than from living men. The boat touched shore and he jumped out and helped drag it up onto the beach.

The village of Fenby was only a few families. The women and children came down from the cluster of huts on the shore to unload the fish. When that was done the old fisherman took Bjarni to a hut made of wood and branches woven together into dense tight walls. With a hammer and a stone they banged and twisted at the chains until they broke the links off Bjarni's wrists.

"You may sleep here," the fisherman said, "and share our fire."

The hut was one large room. Along the walls the people slept; two sheep and a pig were penned in the center. During the day, all the villagers cleaned and cut and salted the fish. Everyone worked at it. Soon Bjarni knew the villagers as if he had always lived with them.

The old fisherman had a daughter named Gifu, barely thirteen. She was thin and tall, red-headed, her white skin scattered with freckles. One day Bjarni came into the hut and found her father thrashing her with a switch.

Bjarni went by them to the corner of the hut where he slept. He had to stoop under the roofbeams.

"Slut," the old man shouted. "If I see you near a man again I will sell you to the Vikings."

"I did nothing," Gifu cried. "I did not kiss him—"

Bjarni left the hut again, to get away from the quarrel. He went out across the village. The villagers were hurrying around to their last chores of the day. A boy was driving in the sheep and pigs. Bjarni wandered around looking at the huts; he was taller than any of them.

To the inland side of the village was a black swamp. He walked along the edge of the solid ground. At one end of the village a path ran off across the marsh. The old fisherman came up to him.

"Bear, where did you say you came from?"

"Iceland."

"I have never heard of it. But you are obviously a fisherman."

"We fish, somewhat." Bjarni combed his fingers through his beard. He nodded down the path into the marsh.

"Where does this trail go?"

"Across the fen," said the old man. "You can stay here with us, if you want."

"Where does it end?"

"It meets the Great Road that goes to York. Stay with us, and I will give you my daughter for your wife."

Bjarni was looking down the track that led through the swamp. "I would rather go to York."

"Well, you can't go now," the fisherman said, disgruntled. "The road is drowned in the winter."

They were facing out over the swamp. Behind them the fisherman's wife called them to supper. Bjarni said, "When will it be passable?"

"In the spring. When the rain stops."

Bjarni turned back toward the village. He and the old fisherman went across the village to their supper.

THE WINTER RAIN FELL. Bjarni and the old fisherman mended the nets and the long lines. The fisherman wanted to use Sigurd's chain as a weight for his nets, but Bjarni would not. He hung it on the wall of the hut beside the straw tick where he slept. The rain stopped. With the other villagers Bjarni went across the sound to a wooded island and cut wood. He left his silver amulet behind. When he returned, it was gone. He guessed that Gifu, the fisherman's daughter, had taken it, and by threats of force made her give it back to him. A few days after that, she asked him for a favor.

"Come with me across the village," she said. "Just to the edge of the fen."

It had been raining; Bjarni was tired of being inside. He put on his shoes and went across the village with her.

"Have you ever been to York?" he asked her.

"York! That is a thousand miles away."

They were passing an open shed. Two boys stood behind the streaming eave. They stared at Gifu, who pretended not to see them. She slid her arm under Bjarni's arm.

"Let go of me," he said.

"Just a while longer, please, Bear."

"Now."

Ahead the ground sank down to the slime of the marsh. She glanced behind them and took her hand from his. "Thank you," she said. He stood looking out across the swamp. The water was black as bog-iron. Gifu went away, leaving him there in the rain.

When Bjarni had been in Fenby almost two months, a boy ran into the village shouting that he had seen a host of longships sailing up the coast from the south.

The villagers met in a crowd on the shore. They listened to the news and wailed. The old fisherman said to Bjarni, "It must be Sigurd Clench-Fist."

Bjarni stood looking over the heads of the other villagers at the panting boy. Between breaths the boy was describing the host that he had seen.

"Yes," Bjarni said. "It sounds like Sigurd's fleet. But many fewer than when I saw him last." He lifted his eyes toward the sea, gladdened. He blessed his fate that was bringing Sigurd to him.

The old fisherman called out to his people. He raised his hands, and the other villagers turned to listen. He said, "Now, we shall not run in panic. Everyone must gather food and clothing for himself, and we shall drive the beasts back into the fen a ways and wait there until Sigurd has gone by."

The villagers rushed off to their huts. Bjarni said, "Why are you running from a name?"

"Don't be foolish," the old fisherman said. "There are but eighteen grown men in Fenby. We are not warriors."

He turned and walked across the village toward his hut. Bjarni walked beside him, talking.

"Sigurd must have been beaten in his war. Otherwise he would winter over in the south. Half his ships are gone."

"One of his ships could take Fenby," the old man said, without missing a stride. He ducked through the door of his home. Before Bjarni could follow, the goodwife came out, a fat bundle of clothing over her shoulder.

"Bring your blanket," she said to Bjarni. "And your chain. They will steal that too."

"I am not running from Sigurd," Bjarni said.

She stared at him a moment and turned back to the door. "Then I will take your blanket."

Bjarni went down to the beach. A rime of ice lay along the tide line. The people of the village crowded off down the swampy path, their belongings on their backs, and their few sheep and pigs trudging behind them. The rain began again.

Bjarni went around the deserted village. Every few steps his eyes turned toward the sea.

The fishermen had left their nets and boats on the beach. In a rowboat he towed the big fishing boat out into the middle of the sound and anchored her fast. The smaller boats he spaced on either side, stretching from one shore to the other. He hung the nets between them. On the beach he piled wood to last the night and built a fire. He took sticks and planted them in the sand, above the tide line, like a flimsy fence. He scavenged around the huts, found nests of dry seaweed and tinder, and heaps of old shells, and the dung of beasts.

The dry tinder and the dung he collected in a place out of the rain. He strung the shells together and hung them up in the wind, between the stakes, and the wind blew them about and made them clatter together.

Around nightfall, Gifu walked out of the swamp.

"I've come to help you," she said.

"Help me?" he asked. "What can you do to help me?"

"I don't know, but I will try," she said. "I promise."

He shook his head at her. The fire burned high, hissing in the rain. He gathered up the tinder he had kept dry and fastened bunches of it to the heads of the stakes, and set them each on fire. The foul night settled down around him. In gusts of wind the shells clacked and banged together. He went up to the hut and took the chain from the wall, and he sat beside the fire with the doubled chain at his feet, waiting for Sigurd.

Gifu huddled in the warmth of the fire, a ragged blanket over her head. She watched him expectantly. He said nothing. He had not asked for her presence and whatever happened to her was her own doing. With his finger he traced runes in the sand. He spelled Hiyke's name. The night gloom was wild with the wind. Only the firelight broke the darkness, and the flames of the torches, laid out flat in the wind.

Around midnight Gifu reached out her hand toward the sea.

"There."

He straightened up to his feet. In the rain he could barely see the barrier of boats and nets he had made across the water. He went back a few paces, away from the flames, to see better.

The wind rose. All around the beach the shells clanged like armor in the darkness. He blinked the rain from his eyes.

Something dark moved out on the water, past the line of boats. His straining ears caught the grinding of oars in their oarlocks. A longship was rowing up the sound.

Now he could make out the mass of the other ships of Sigurd's fleet, clustered beyond the low island where he had met the fishermen. The longship sent in to scout had to put up her oars. A light burned in her waist. Tentatively the ship nosed forward again, turning to row along the barrier.

Bjarni wiped the rain out of his eyes. Something touched his elbow. Gifu had followed him; she stood beside him, shivering, her hand on his arm. Together they watched the longship row back out to meet the other ships beyond the island. Those ships began to move.

"They are going away," Gifu murmured.

The fleet glided away to the north. Bjarni watched until they were gone.

"Why did they go?" Gifu said. "They could have broken through the nets with the prows of their ships."

"Once you start to run away, you never stop," Bjarni said.

He went back to the fire, the chain swinging in his

hand, and sat down in the warmth of the flames. The English girl sat beside him. She leaned against him, her head against his arm. He stared into the fire, curling up from the charred wood, popping and sparkling in the rain. He was running away from Hiyke Ragnarsdottir. He reached out for another piece of wood and put it on the fire. At that moment he decided to go back to Hrafn-fell.

IN THE LASHING SLEET of the late winter he dug the good-wife's garden for her, and when the first spring sun began to shine he planted it. The other men fished for salmon in the rocky streams along the coast. The air warmed in the sunlight. A fresh southern breeze began to blow, a light, female wind. Bjarni took the chain down off the wall, and the goodwife gave him a sack of food; she wept, saying good-bye, which startled him. The white-bearded fisherman walked with him to the path.

"Be careful. The road is dangerous. Watch for thieves."

"I will," Bjarni said. He shook the old man's hand and started away.

"Be wary of the Normans," the old man called. "They are wicked men."

Bjarni waved to him. He hung his bundle on his back; his feet sank into the stinking black earth of the swamp.

"Bear," the old man shouted. "At the Rowan Ford. There is a robber there."

Bjarni raised his arm over his head, without turning. He did not look back again. He walked on through the swamp, going southeast.

The day was fair. He cut a stout stick from a clump of trees and walked with it. The path led him all that morning through black swamp just coming to bud. The sun rode high in the sky. The path left the swamp and crossed a ridge crowded with brambles and bees. The trail met another, wider road, with ruts from the wheels of carts. This led down a hillside. At the bottom of the slope, the road crossed a stream running shallow over a broad field of pebbles. On the far side of the stream stood a tree with a trunk like a silver column.

Bjarni stopped at the edge of the water. He had never seen a rowan tree before, but in the stories he had heard since his childhood the rowan was a great tree. He had the chain over his shoulder, and he closed his hand on it. At a steady pace he went across the stream.

The water was clear as spring water. It hardly dampened his shoes. He was halfway to the far side when a man shouted at him to stand. A man on a bay horse rode out of the forest beyond the rowan tree.

Bjarni walked on across the stream. The rider swung his horse to bar the way by the rowan. He was a big man, although not of Bjarni's size. He wore a coat of metal links and carried a long-handled axe.

"Nobody crosses here," he said to Bjarni, "unless they pay me a toll."

"I have nothing," Bjarni said. "And I am already across."

The horseman reined his snorting horse back to keep between Bjarni and the path. "That chain looks sound," he said. "I will take that."

"This I will give to you," Bjarni said. He swung the chain off his shoulder; he whipped it around the knees of the horse and yanked its forelegs out from under it.

The rider jumped off. He brought his axe around at Bjarni's head. Bjarni dropped to his knees and the axe flew over him. He dropped the end of the chain and hit the robber in the face.

Blood spurted from the robber's nose. He raised the axe again and Bjarni hit him full in the face with all his might.

The robber fell over backward. His thrashing horse kicked him. He lay still on the road. The horse was struggling to rise, the chain still coiled around its legs. Bjarni freed it and chased it off down the road.

The robber lay on his back, his head in a puddle of blood. Bjarni bent over him. He was dead. Either the blows or the horse's kick had killed him.

Bjarni wrapped the chain around the robber's chest and hung him up in the rowan tree, which was Thor's tree. Kneeling down before the tree he prayed that the god should see what Bjarni offered in his honor. He swore to the Thunderer to keep faith.

He went on down the road, through a wood of thin white trees on whose branches the green buds were bursting open. His mood was dark; his hand hurt, and his thoughts kept turning to the robber. He wished that he knew whether he himself had killed him or the horse had done it, kicking him. He had never slain anyone. Always before, after the fight was over the fighters got up and shook hands, smiling, sometimes forcing the smile.

The road met another road and widened again, and now a river ran alongside it, and thick-trunked trees grew up on the banks. Night was creeping down from the sky. He would have to find a place to sleep. A sound reached him from back up the road, a clopping rhythm. He looked back and saw the robber's bay horse galloping after him.

All his hair stood on end. The twilight masked the rider on the horse's back. He stepped off the road into the high grass. The horse slowed; its eyes were white-rimmed and bulging.

"Bear!"

It was Gifu. He let his muscles go slack. "What are you doing here?" he said.

"I'm going with you," she said.

He shook his head and stepped onto the road again. "Go on—go home."

The horse walked after him. From its back, she spoke to him, spoke over him. "I'm not going home. Even if I don't go with you, I am never going home again."

He said nothing to that. When the night fell and she was hungry, she would go home. They walked along together. The sky darkened, and he left the road. Putting his bundle down under a tree he built a fire.

"Did you bring anything to eat?" she said.

"Only enough for me."

"Oh."

He sat beside his little fire, no larger than his cupped hands. The wind rattled the branches of the tree together over his head. He took bread from his bundle and ate. The girl watched, her mouth open, her bony arms pebbled with gooseflesh from the cold.

"I will buy bread," she said.

"I don't want what you have to pay me with."

"I have money." She took a leather purse from the front of her dress and spilled it out onto the grass. A dozen silver coins slid into the firelight.

"By Thor's howe," Bjarni said. He put his hand out to the shining coins.

She sat back smiling. He did not touch the money. It was the robber's money. She had robbed the corpse. He stared at her, angry, until she stopped smiling and her eyes grew wary.

"Did you leave him where he hung?"

"I didn't—" Her hand moved across her body, up and down, back and forth, the Christian sign. "I didn't touch him. On the horse, the purse was. In the horse's saddlebag."

Bjarni grunted. He fed dry grass to the fire. His fingers were swollen. The chain had printed his fingers with bruises.

"Bear?" she said. "I'm hungry. Will you give me something to eat?"

He flung the rest of the loaf at her to quiet her. She broke off a piece and toasted it on a stick in the fire.

THE ROAD FLOWED into another road, broad as eight horses abreast; the ruts worn in it streamed with water. They walked down the side where the ground was dry. Gifu rode the horse, her legs dangling down the saddle, and her feet far above the stirrups. Bjarni did not speak to her; he still hoped that she would go home. Yet he fed her. Her family had sheltered him and when she begged he had to give her food.

The forest yielded to a high windy moor. The road dented it like a crease running through the grass. Tracks showed in the mud of the road: deer tracks, dog tracks, and later in the day the track of a horse's hoof. They slept in the ditch at night.

After a few days they walked into a village of three little huts around a well. The wives of the place sat around the well; they let Bjarni draw up the bucket and water Gifu's horse and drink.

"How far is it to York?" he asked.

The women laughed and shook their heads at him; when they spoke he could barely understand one word in five. Gifu's people had spoken with an accent, but these people's speech was outlandish to him. He did not try to talk to them again. Gifu hung back from them.

The men of the place came in from the fields. Night was falling. Bjarni felt the sack. There was nothing left of the food Gifu's mother had given to him when he left Fenby.

Gifu was sitting on the edge of the well behind him. He got hold of her and pulled her down. The robber's purse was in her bodice. He stuck his hand down past her breast for it.

"Hey!" she cried. "That's my money!"

Bjarni counted all the silver, except one coin, back into the purse and shoved it under his belt. He took the sack off across the green of the village. Gifu screamed curses at him from the well.

Two oxen grazed at the edge of the green, near the biggest of the three huts. There were heaps of garbage around it and firewood stacked as high as the roofbeam by the door. Voices came through the open doorway. On the threshold sat an old woman, her teeth gone, and her nose hooked, talking to herself. Tufts of white hair poked out under her scarf.

Bjarni stood before the doorway and called. A woman in middle years came out of the hut, brushing past the crone in the doorway. Bjarni held out the sack. He made signs with his hands to show that he wanted food; he showed the goodwife the silver coin. Her eyes widened. From her own hut she carried the sack around to the other two and came back with two long loaves of bread, a wedge of cheese, and some onions and turnips. Bjarni argued a little, and she added a sausage. He gave her the coin and went back to the well.

Gifu sat with her back to the edge of the well, her arms wrapped around her knees. "You'd better give me back my money," she said.

He gave her a bit of the cheese and some of the bread. They sat together eating. The wind was coming up, and the well sheltered them. Up over them the stars began to prick through the darkness of the sky. He lay down on the grass, his arms behind his head. The memory of Hiyke sprang into his mind. He would see her again; he was eager to think of her. The wind stirred the grass around him. He would tell all this to Hiyke: when he was home, he would make poems to tell everyone.

"Look at that," Gifu said. "I hope they don't bother us."

Three or four boys in a little group moved along the far end of the green. Their voices grew louder. They threw rocks at the oxen and the great cattle lumbered away.

Gifu asked, "Will they throw stones at my horse?" Standing up, she went off through the windy grass toward the horse, midway to the nearest of the huts. Bjarni lay back again. He watched the stars. They were different here. The summer square, just rising, was nearly in the arch of the sky.

"Hey!"

The shout brought him up to a sit. The boys, indistinct in the dark, had come up the meadow and were throwing rocks at the old woman in the doorway of the hut. It was Gifu who had shouted. She ran forward, shouting again, and bent for a rock and threw it at the boys.

They turned on her. She squatted down and coolly dug rocks up from the grass and flung them much better than the boys did. One of them yelped, and another ran away.

The two remaining hurried after him. Gifu rose from the grass. The door of the hut opened and the hag was taken in. Gifu came back to Bjarni.

"Here," he said, and gave her an onion.

She sat beside him to eat it. He lay down again to watch the stars.

"Bear?"

"Yes."

"Where are we going?"

He lay still a moment, the starlight in his eyes. At length, he said, "We are both going home—you to Fenby."

"I am never going home. Where is your home?"

"Iceland."

"Iceland! What is that—a country made of ice?"

He did not answer. His beard itched and he scratched through the wiry hair at his chin.

"Where is it? Iceland."

He pointed to the North Star. "Almost directly beneath that star."

She sat up, leaning against him, to see the star he was pointing toward; she looked along his arm. "That's at the edge of the world." She bit into the onion. "How will you get there?"

"Over the sea. But it is not at the edge of the world— Iceland is at the center of the world, or very near."

"Then why have I never heard of it?"

"You have never heard of anyplace," he said. He pointed to the North Star again. "That star, you see, we call the Millstem. The world is a mill, with the sky as the upper millstone, and the land and sea as the nether millstone.

Only a few days' sail north from Iceland, the sea rushes down through the hole in the nether millstone, which is at the center, of course."

She was eating the onion. "That is un-so. The center of the world is Jerusalem, as everyone knows, where Jesus was nailed to the Cross."

"I am going to sleep," he said. It was a mistake to talk to her, to enjoy her company. She would get him in trouble. He lay down and put his head in his arms.

THE CITY OF YORK was by a river that emptied into the sea, and seafaring ships were anchored there, moored up in rows between the banks where sheep grazed. There were no ships from Iceland. Bjarni spoke to such of the sailors as he could find to understand him, and they told him that a Danish ship could take him home. Most of the ships were Frisian, come to load English wool. He did not find a Danish ship.

He walked back along the riverbank to the city. A great stone wall surrounded it, but the city itself had shrunk down to a few crooked streets in the middle, with a stone tower standing over them. Elsewhere were older houses, deserted and burned, and streets overgrown with brambles.

Gifu said, "The Normans came here. That's why the tower is there. To keep order. They burned everything. There were rebels and they hanged them."

She and Bjarni were walking along a cobbled street slimy with the excrement of dogs and goats. The buildings on either side were built out over the street, penning the air under them until it was too foul to breathe. Other people crowded by. He stretched his legs toward the place where the street widened.

Her horse was grazing where they had left it, on a hillside near the wall. Bjarni sat down on the grass. The ruins of a house covered the flat ground below him. Lifting his head, he could see another on the slope above him. There were more ruins here than living houses. The wall was old and crumbling. This had been a great place once. He sat thinking of the Normans who had destroyed it.

Gifu was rubbing down the horse with a handful of grass. She talked to it and sang to it. Bjarni rose and went over to her and said, "The sailors here tell me that I will find a ship in London to take me home."

Busily she scrubbed dried mud from the horse's foreleg. "Where is London?"

"At the other end of the Great Road." He scratched the horse under the jaw and it groaned and pushed its head out, enjoying the caress. The girl crouched almost at Bjarni's feet. He said, "You've come far enough, now, Gifu. You must go back to Fenby."

She shook her head. "I am never going home. I have told you that."

"I don't know how far London is—I don't know what I might find there. I can't care for you. Go home. Take the horse."

"My father will switch me."

"He will only beat you once."

She was working over the horse's leg. The back of her neck was grey with dirt. Lice crawled in her fuzzy red hair. She said, "He will switch me every day. When he finds out I am with child, he will whip me to death."

"By the nine howes," he said.

She turned on him like an animal, hooking her fingers into his clothes. "Take me with you. I can't go home. I have no place to go except with you."

He recoiled. She smelled strongly of sweat and female humors. He pulled her hands out of his clothes and she caught hold of him again, and two dirty tears rolled down her cheeks.

"Please," she cried.

"Gifu, I cannot take you with me."

She wept, clutching him, and when he backed away from her she let him drag her after. He stood still, afraid of stepping on her. She wept and rubbed her face against his thigh.

"Gifu," he said. "Stop."

She wailed. He relented; bending down into the ripe field of her smells he lifted her and put her on the horse. He took the horse by the bridle and led it down through York toward the Great Road. She snuffled, making a great display of wiping her eyes, but he caught a glimpse of her when she thought he could not see, and she was smiling. He wondered if she had gulled him. Uncertain, he led her on down the road toward London.

. . .

THEY LEFT THE FLAT MOORS behind and traveled through a forest that seemed endless. The sky was hemmed down to a narrow strip over his head, and when the wind blew the trees rubbed their branches together, squeaking and banging, with all the leaves rustling, in a racket that unsettled him. The day after they left York, they came on a river.

Bjarni went along it away from the road. The river curved. A tree had fallen into the water just above the bend, and in its lee was a deep quiet pool. He took off his clothes and dove into the water.

Gifu sat on the bank in the sun and watched him. He scrubbed himself with handfuls of river sand. His skin tingled and glowed red under the scrubbing; light-hearted, he sang:

> *Bless the giant's daughter*
> *That spills you onto the ground*

Gifu sat frowning at him from the riverbank. "Why do you do that—go naked in the water?"

"To get clean," he said.

"I would never do that."

"You will," he said, "now." He started toward her, pushing through water up to his waist.

She leapt up and ran toward the horse, hitched to a tree downstream. Bjarni chased her. He thought at first that she was making a game of it, but when he caught her she scratched him and tried to kick him between the legs. She bit him. She was frightened. He held her still, with one knee on her waist pinning her to the ground, and peeled off her clothes. She fought, her breath seething through her clenched teeth. Her body was still adolescent. Under her filthy white skin lay ribs delicate as a child's. He dragged her into the water and washed her hair, picking out the vermin clustered around her nape and crown, and scrubbed her skin clean.

He let her go on the bank. Before she was dry she scrambled back into her rags of shift and dress and hose. Bjarni sat down on the grass to let the wind dry him.

"You bastard," she shouted. "You whore's son. I hope a snake eats you. Let the Great Snake eat you! I hope you drown. I hope you hang."

"If you are coming with me, Gifu, stay clean."

She called him more names and gave him more wishes for his death. Running out of wind, she stood staring at him. Her skin was like milk; her drying hair gleamed. Under her gaze he put his clothes on.

"You are not going to do anything," she said.

He started back along the stream toward the road. She ran ahead of him to the horse and climbed into the saddle. He watched the river; among the mossy stones something gleamed at him, faded and gleamed again, a fish. Gifu's horse crashed through the high grass after him.

"I'm sorry. I thought you were going to. You know."

"What?"

"You know."

The brambles tore at his clothes, his bare forearms.
They reached the road, higher than the land around it.

"Why don't you want me?" she said. "Am I too ugly?"

"I love someone else," he said.

The horse clopped along beside him, its head lowered.
She held the reins in her fists. Bjarni put one hand on the
thick mane of the horse.

"The road is good here. I'll run until I get tired, and
you can ride along."

"Who is she? Is she of Fenby?"

He broke into a run. The horse loped heavily along
beside him. They went at his best pace along the road,
through the shade of the trees.

THEY CAME TO A TOWN on a height of land above a little
river. The plain below the town was busy with swarms
of people. Booths of stone and turf stood here and there
on the meadow, and people were unloading wagons and
talking and making games.

Curious, Bjarni went around the field, stopping before
each of the booths to look over what was happening
there. He kept his hand on his wallet. In crowds there
were always thieves. A boy passed him, trailing a stink
of goat. The meadow grass turned swampy under Bjarni's
feet, and he veered back toward higher ground.

The stone and turf walls of the booths reminded him
of the booths at Thingvellir in Iceland, where the Althing

was held; but here the booths had been spread with goods for sale and show. There were stacks of cloth for sale, and pots, iron, cheese, trays of fragrant bread, jewelry and hides and bunches of herbs, and an ale-shop. After the quiet of the road he enjoyed the noise and the jostling crowds. He passed a man and a woman on horseback talking in a nasal language he guessed was Norman French. Beside an empty wagon, three young men lounged in the grass, tootling on pipes, patting a little drum. Bjarni paused to listen. A girl rushed by him, laughing, flowers wound in her dark hair.

Other young people joined them. Bjarni moved out of their way. They danced, the boys in a ring facing in, their hands joined, and the girls in a ring in the middle facing out. The dance was simple, three steps, a few kicks, and a turn; then they stopped and everyone kissed. Bjarni laughed. He went off toward the ale-shop.

Gifu reappeared beside him on her horse. He walked slowly around the field, his hand on his wallet. She followed him, her reins slack.

"See what I found." She held out a length of green ribbon.

"Found or stole?"

She shrugged, admiring the ribbon in her hand. "I will put my hair in it. Here. Help me." She gave him the ribbon and slid down from her saddle. Gathering her hair in her hand, she turned her back to him.

While he was fastening the ribbon around her hair, three or four horsemen rode by, shouting in French. They wore their hair long as women's, and ribbons fluttered on their hats and full sleeves.

"Normans," Gifu said. She patted her hair down. "They say the Jarl of Lincoln is here. Maybe the king, even."

Bjarni was looking back at the ale-shop. The tankard he had drunk there was making him thirsty. He said, "Don't steal anymore. You will get yourself in trouble." He went back toward the booth, swarming with people.

Gifu led her horse after him, and he bought her a tankard as well, and two loaves. They sat on the grass watching the crowd. Normans studded it, riding, their gaudy clothes and the harness of their horses chiming with bells.

In the afternoon a sudden storm turned the plain to a mire. The last daylight dried off enough of the ground to let a dust cloud rise. Hoarding his money, Bjarni stopped drinking, fell sober, and got a headache. Night came. The people lit bonfires and danced around them. They made noisy love in the grass. Gifu left her horse with Bjarni, making him promise to watch over it, and went to join in the dancing, the drinking, the laughing. Bjarni tethered the horse to a tree and fell asleep beside it.

He woke in the deep night. Girls were singing nearby him. He sat up. A line of boys and girls was snaking around the field, holding torches and singing; the boys answered the girls. They danced off into the wood. Bjarni sat watching until they returned a few moments later. The two girls leading the parade bore a birch tree over their heads. All the branches had been cut off save a few at the top. They carried the tree all over the field and at last put it on end in the ground and fixed it fast with stones.

Bjarni slept again. When he woke, Gifu was sitting beside him, yawning. She smelled of flowers.

"Look there," she said.

Arm in arm, a dozen young men and girls were crossing the plain toward them. They sang at the top of their lungs. After them came a creature made of leaves, strutting from side to side. Green boughs covered it from its pointed head to the ground. It wore a red cloak and a wooden crown, and as it went along it waved its leafy arms solemnly from side to side.

"The King of the Green," Gifu cried. "Let's go get his blessing."

She towed Bjarni by the hand in the wake of the procession. The King of the Green circled the field behind his singing court. They passed two Normans on tall horses, who trotted forward to block the leaf-king's way. They were laughing. The King of the Green bowed so deeply that his wickerwork frame tipped and Bjarni, behind him, saw his muddy stockings. One of the Norman knights swept off his belled hat in answer. His shining hair slid down over his shoulders. Laughing, he turned his horse and cantered away. The King of the Green did not move; he looked uncertain, sapped of his royalty. Gifu swung around, her hand on her stomach.

"I am hungry." She glanced at Bjarni, sly, over her shoulder.

Bjarni's stomach was empty. He touched his wallet,

reluctant to spend more money. He turned the back of his head to her, saying nothing. She skipped away. The King of the Green moved off again, heralded by singers.

Gifu returned. Her sleeves bulged.

"Do you know who that was? Who met the May-King? It was the real king! It was Red William."

Bjarni scanned the crowd. The long-haired Norman was far across the plain. He had heard odd talk of him, even away in Iceland. Gifu poked a long cake into his hand.

"Eat."

He let her feed him. They walked past a woman selling milk from a bucket. Gifu's cheeks bulged with sweet cakes.

"He went up to the May-King for a blessing, neat as a monk selling pardons." She shook her head. "As if he deserved it. Such as him. By rights not a seed should sprout in England while he is king."

It was true, then, what he had heard of Red William. Ahead were several shouting boys. Bjarni swerved his course to look beyond them. In the midst of boisterous people were two men sitting on a bench with their feet and hands and heads in stocks. The little mob around them pelted them with dirt and stones. He took Gifu by the arm and pulled her away.

"Where are you going?" she asked.

"I should not let you steal."

She laughed. Squirming out of his grip, she ran away across the plain toward her horse.

Near the ale-shop there was a grey wolf chained to a tree. A loose ring of men stood watching it. A stout stick was bound between its jaws. The wolf lay with its head on its paws, its back to the tree. Every few moments it snarled in a low rumble like stones rolled in a keg.

"That's the biggest wolf in England," said a man nearby.

Bjarni had never seen a wolf before. "It looks of an ordinary size to me."

The man strode up to him. "That wolf could take down a horse." He was drunk, and head and shoulders shorter than Bjarni.

"I could take down a horse," Bjarni said. "I could take down that wolf."

"You're mad."

Bjarni took his wallet from his belt and jangled it.

"Mad." The Englishman wheeled. "Hear! Listen to this —this fool says he will fight my wolf."

The other men pressed around them. The Englishman whose wolf it was sneered up at Bjarni.

"Now shake your purse at me."

Bjarni opened his wallet, took out six shillings, and passed them under the Englishman's nose.

"By yourself," the Englishman said. "With no weapon."

The others began to argue if it could be done. The Englishman stuck out his hand to Bjarni and they shook on the wager.

More men were crowding around the tree. Gifu had ridden her horse over behind them to watch him. The

Englishman called for help. He and two others used a heavy staff with a fork at one end to pin the wolf to the ground and took the stick from between its jaws.

The wolf lunged up, throwing its weight against the staff, and knocked it aside, and the Englishmen scurried out of the way. The wolf reared against its chain. Its growls made the watching women shriek.

Smiling, the Englishman strutted over to Bjarni again. "Think once more, big man."

Bjarni tossed his wallet over the heads of the crowd to Gifu. He hitched his belt up with his thumbs. To the Englishmen, he said, "After I go within the chain's length of the tree, if I leave again without winning, the bet's lost."

"You are mad."

"What are you doing?" Gifu cried.

Bjarni walked up to the wolf. It crouched back, baring its teeth. Its yellow eyes were like beacons. When he came within its range it flew at him. He ran past it, jumped across the swinging chain, and as the wolf wheeled to meet him gripped its fur with one hand, behind the ear.

The beast snapped at him. Its breath reeked. He lifted it off the ground at arm's length. It was much heavier than he had expected. He seized its tail with his free hand and laid the wolf down on its side between two roots of the tree and put his knee on its shoulder. With the other hand he held its head to the ground.

"Enough?" he said to the Englishman.

The little man was wagging his head from side to side. "Enough," he said. "You have won."

They put the stick between the beast's jaws again and tied it, and Bjarni let it go. The Englishman paid him. The watching crowd boomed with deafening cheers. A fat woman plowed through the fringe of people and kissed him.

"Come into the bushes, dear, I want a taste of that myself!"

Gifu clutched his arm. He got the wallet back from her and put the money into it. Fists pounded on his back and shoulders and hands waved around him, trying to touch him, and passing tankards up to him. He drank off three cups of ale as they came to him. A horseman wedged his way through the crowd and shouted at him in French.

Bjarni tucked his wallet into his belt. He turned away from the rider, whom he could not understand. Another woman gave him ale and he drank.

"Bear," Gifu cried. "Didn't you hear him?" Her face was pink. "He's from the king. He has a message from the king, Bear!"

He lowered the flagon of ale. Beyond the waving arms and heads, the fair-haired Norman king was watching him from the back of his horse. Their eyes met. King William smiled. Bjarni gulped down the rest of the ale.

DRUNKEN, LAUGHING, the flower-decked boys and girls hauled the King of the Green by his hands down to the river and threw him in. They cheered.

"When will you see the king?" Gifu asked. She turned her horse away from the river.

"At sunset."

"I'll go with you."

"No."

"Oh, you must. You must let me go. Please?" Leaping down from the saddle she clutched his arm and hung on him. "Please?"

He pushed her away.

"It isn't fair!" she cried.

The King of the Green was trying to swim across the river. The wickerwork costume buoyed him up so high he could not make headway across the current. His court jeered at him from the bank. Bjarni started along the plain toward the road. He had not decided yet if he wanted to meet the king.

Gifu trotted after him, towing the horse. "Are you going there like that?"

He looked down at his hide coat. "I am covered," he said.

"You look like a common lout," she said. "A serf."

"What would you have me do? Twist some branches together?"

"Come with me," she said.

He followed her up a narrow track in the hill toward the town on its summit. Bjarni could not remember its name; Gifu knew the town as if she had always lived there. She took him through the wooden gate into the city and led him down the streets that wound along the hilltop until she came to an inn. While he stood in the doorway of the common room, she went around the place demanding to speak with the innkeeper.

Fat and bald, the innkeeper came into the common room. "Who are you?"

Gifu put her hands on her hips and stuck out her chin. "Now, mark me, I shall say this only once. The king has summoned—has asked my master to wait upon him. You see him there. Probably you saw his deed today with the wolf. We are far from home—strangers here. We shall need your best bed. In a room. And a fair meal, when we have seen the king."

Bjarni slid his thumbs under his belt. At the heavy tables around the room, the men had lifted their chins out of their alebowls to stare at him. The innkeeper blinked at him.

Gifu clapped her hands together. She stalked past the innkeeper to shout at him again. "Hurry! The king waits even now to speak to him. We have great news for him —signs, omens. We must make ready."

The innkeeper bustled to his work. "This way." Bowing, he led Bjarni up the plank stairs and took him along the corridor at the top to a small room with a bed and a window. Gifu strutted around it.

"Well. This will do, for the while." She returned to the innkeeper, whose bulk filled the doorway. "Now. He will need fit clothing." She tugged on the innkeeper's brown coat. "This will serve."

The innkeeper hesitated only a moment. He said, "The

king." Stripping off his coat, he held it out to Bjarni, who put it on. The coat caught him under the arms. He stretched his shoulders carefully.

"We are of a size," the innkeeper said, smiling, to Gifu.

She gestured vaguely under his nose. "If you say so. We want a good meal, now, remember. A roast, and a soup, and a stew—pies—"

Bjarni went past the innkeeper to the door. "Make the bed," he told her. He left the room.

THE KING OF THE ENGLISH was in his middle age. His chair was carved with dancing lions. At his right hand was a Norse priest in a black gown, who translated what was said.

"His grace the king welcomes you to his kingdom, to his city of Lincoln, and to his court."

Bjarni thanked him.

"His grace asks your name and your lord's name."

"I am Bjarni Hoskuldsson, and I am Icelandic. We are all equals in my country; I have no lord."

The king fondled his shining yellow hair. His pale eyes bulged, set wide apart, intelligent. He spoke.

"His grace asks how you came to England."

Bjarni did not want to tell him that. He said, "I was shipwrecked."

The king sat back in the deep chair. He put one foot on a stool before him. The boot was caked with yellow mud. He and the priest talked back and forth in French. The king seized eagerly on something the priest said.

"His grace wishes to know if you play chess."

"I play chess," Bjarni said.

"Then his grace will have a game with you."

Pages brought in a table with a checkerboard top and a box of men. Bjarni and the king played a game of some twenty-five moves, and Bjarni won.

The king looked angry. The high color rose in his cheeks. It was for that he was named the Red, not for his hair.

"His grace says you play excellently well."

Bjarni said, "Chess is our delight, in Iceland. Chess and law. The king plays a good game."

"He seldom loses."

"He is the king." Bjarni began to put away the chessmen in their box. They were carved of stone, and even the pawns had faces. He had never seen so fine a set, not even Eirik Arnarson's.

"His grace asks if you have a king in Iceland."

"No. As I said, we are free men there."

The Norse priest frowned at him. "The King of Norway is your rightful ruler."

"Is he?" Bjarni shut the lid of the chess box. "I have never met him."

The king tapped the priest impatiently on the arm. The priest listened to a flight of words in French.

"His grace wishes you to join his court."

"I am on my way home to Iceland."

"You could serve no greater prince than King William. He is king of England, duke in all but name of Normandy, overlord of Scotland and Ireland. Soon he will overmaster France. There will be a new Emperor in Europe, with no Pope to share his honor and his power."

Bjarni bowed his head slightly to the Norman on the throne. "Then I wish him good fortune."

To his surprise the king laughed. He made some remarks to the priest.

"You will stay at least awhile. His grace will see that you are lodged and kept. You and your lady wife. Perhaps he will help you on your way home again. You are dismissed—he will expect you at court tomorrow."

Bjarni stood silent before the king; he had intended to take the road again that evening. Yet his fate had brought him here for some purpose. He nodded to the king.

"Tell him I will come."

The king raised his eyebrows at him, looking half-surprised, and spoke through his nose to the priest. The Norseman said, "You should kneel before his grace."

Bjarni said, "I would not ask him to kneel before me." He went to the door and let himself out. On the landing of the stairs, just outside, he heard the king laugh.

WHEN HE RETURNED to the inn, Gifu had a table set in their little room. She made him sit down at it, and with a shoeless child to help her she brought in the dinner. Bjarni fell to eating. He kept the little boy running back and forth for ale. Midway through the meal, the boy dropped the pitcher and it broke. Gifu slapped him.

"What a mess!"

The boy knelt to mop up the spill. Bjarni said, "Leave him alone, Gifu. Come and eat."

She had gone for a broom; she swept the pieces of the pitcher into a heap. "Don't you dare offend him," she said to the child. "He is a sorcerer. He walked up out of the sea after a terrible storm. When the Vikings came, he cast a spell over our whole village, and the Vikings ran away."

The boy threw a white look at Bjarni. He mumbled something. Bjarni sat back, the remnants of his dinner littering the table before him. Gifu sat on the stool opposite him and stuffed food into her mouth. The child crept toward the door.

"Here." Bjarni stood, picked up the boy by the arm, and set him down on the chair. "Eat." He went down the stairs to the common room of the inn and found another pitcher of ale.

He climbed the stairs to the second story and went down the hall to his bedchamber. The scullion had gone, the table was cleared, and Gifu lay on the featherbed, her white arms thrown out. Bjarni shut the door.

"Why do you lie?" he said. *"A sorcerer."*

"It keeps them in their place," Gifu said. "To know I travel with a prince of nature."

In the morning of the day following, Bjarni went up to the castle to the king, expecting to find something akin to the courts of stories: an interminable banquet. Instead he came into a wide bare room stinking hot from the fire on the hearth, where two or three courtiers lounged sleepily in corners. The men were gaudy in long full coats; the one woman had covered her hair with a white linen coif, not a tress showing, and her face was so smoothly painted she seemed like a statue of horn. Bjarni wandered around the hot room awhile, looking at the hangings on the walls. The woven figures in the hangings were more what he expected: men riding to war and building towers and sitting at table. The pretty courtiers were watching him with a drowsy interest. The woman spoke to him in French.

"I speak no French," he said.

She strolled toward him, lifting her skirt in one hand. The men were smiling behind their hands. Bjarni sniffed at the light fragrance of verbena in the air. The woman murmured something and put her hand on his sleeve. Her eyelashes fluttered. She was like no woman he had ever seen, and he looked closer at her and saw she was a man.

He pushed her hand violently away; the three courtiers by the wall shrieked with laughter. The man-woman smiled disdainfully at him and said a long sentence of French that set the other men to roaring with laughter. Bjarni stood lump-footed, his hands at his sides. His face was hot. The woman sauntered away from him, swinging her hips, and gave him a coy look. The courtiers slapped their knees and doubled up over their giggling.

Bjarni stared at them, his blush cooling in his cheeks; he began to be curious. They glared back, taking offense. The woman said something in a honeyed voice and the others laughed obediently. Several other men came into the room.

These were just as strange to Bjarni, three men in middle or ripe age, dressed in black with brimless black caps on their heads. Their beards and the sides of their hair were braided. The first of them spoke in French to the courtiers.

The woman replied. The newcomer glanced at Bjarni and nodded to him and turned back to the courtiers, and they spoke. Bjarni went to the door and down the stairs.

While he was in the yard the three older men in black came down after him, and the leader of them approached him.

"Are you here to see the king? He is hunting. He will be back by nightfall," he said in English. "Are you not the sorcerer?"

"I am not a sorcerer," Bjarni said.

The spare, pale face stretched into a pleasant smile. "Not even a Pythagorean? I am Aaron. You are perhaps Norse?"

Bjarni told him his name and homeland.

"Iceland," Aaron said. "I see the king's interest in you. Aside from your remarkable feat with the wolf. I have heard that in Iceland the summer sun never sets, and the winter sun never rises. Is that so?"

"It goes down and comes right up again," Bjarni said. "The king's interest. He has an odd selection of interests."

"Let no one tell you about the king. I for one will say no word against him. He has protected my people. The Christians may be put off by that."

"You are not Christian?" Bjarni asked.

The old man's look sharpened, intent. "I am a Jew." He motioned toward his black cap and the dressing of his hair.

"I ask you to pardon my ignorance," Bjarni said.

"You may lose your ignorance here," said Aaron. "Are you not a Christian?"

Bjarni marked the crowded yard around them and made no answer. He said, "Thank you. I shall heed your advice." He put out his hand. Aaron touched it with a cold white palm. His hands were smooth and small. He and his friends moved away across the yard, and Bjarni returned to the inn.

THAT NIGHT, when Bjarni was half-asleep, someone slid into the bed with him. At first he thought it was Gifu.

A hard wet mouth came down on his. He smelled verbena. With a swing of his arm he flung the stranger out of the bed.

The room was dark; he could hear Gifu in the corner laughing. The stranger, babbling in French, tried to reach the door. Bjarni got him by the hair, threw open the little window over the bed, and stuffed the Norman out headfirst.

Wailing, the Norman fell down to the yard below. Bjarni

stood on the bed to look after him. Gifu popped up beside him. Half a dozen men were gathered in the yard. The one who had crawled into bed with Bjarni was sitting in the mud under the window. The others fell on him, shrieking, and hauled him away across the dirt to a horse-trough and threw him in.

Gifu laughed again. Bjarni shook his head. "I don't think these people have any shame."

"You are nothing but a farmer."

Down in the yard the Normans were dunking one another successively in the horse-trough. Bjarni pulled the shutter fast over the window and went to bed again, but their screams and yells and laughter kept him awake for another hour.

The next day was rainy, and the king did not hunt. He called Bjarni to play chess. Bjarni won the first two games. The king beat him in the third, and shook Bjarni's hand and took the silver ring from his finger and gave it to him. The Norse priest was there; they spoke through him.

"It is noised about Lincoln that you have certain powers," the king said.

Bjarni was setting up the chessmen again on the board. He said, "All lies."

"You need not put me off," the king said. He leaned on one elbow over the chess-game, his eyes darting from the men to Bjarni's face. "In my kingdom no man suffers for what he honestly believes. You must have seen how I have gathered unusual men around me."

"I have seen it," Bjarni said. "But I am being honest. I have no powers, only the strength of my back."

"You disparage yourself," the king said. "What think you of Jesus Christ?"

As the Norse priest passed on the words, he screwed up his mouth, as if he tasted poison. Bjarni said, "I know little of Christ. Of the Christians, I know a little more, enough not to speak against their god in a place where there are so many of them."

He put his queen's pawn forward, to distract the king with the game. The king put out his same pawn.

"What think you of Moses, and of Mohammed?"

"They are only names to me, names in old stories."

The king's eyes gleamed. He said, "In my opinion, they are all frauds, every one, beguiling the weak-minded with their talk of salvation."

The priest spoke that unwillingly. Bjarni moved out his queen's knight. "If you believe so, then it is true, for you."

"What do you believe?"

"I believe in castling as soon as possible," Bjarni said, "and in attacking on the king's side."

The king laughed. The game was well begun, and they turned their attention to it. There was no more talk of gods. Bjarni won the game. For that, the king gave him no gifts.

AFTERWARD, on the stairs going down, Bjarni came on the Norse priest; he said, "Why do you let him speak such calumnies of your god through you?"

"Ah, you horse-eating pagan," the Norseman said. "It is your fault."

They went down together without speaking again. Then at the door the priest turned to Bjarni.

"He is the king. Only a fool denies the king. You ought to remember that."

He left the tower ahead of Bjarni. They separated, going across the wide crowded yard in the rain.

GIFU HAD TAKEN to straying around the city while Bjarni was at the king's court. One evening she did not come back to the inn.

He went to the reeking stableyard. Her horse was gone. In the late twilight, when the streets were thronged with people coming in from the fields outside the city, he climbed the hill to the Norman tower.

At the back of the tower, above the midden, and far from the great door where the king went in, there was a pen where the city lawmen kept prisoners. Bjarni let himself through the gate. Above the reek of the midden, he smelled hot metal. Ahead, beside the pen, three men were standing at a little fire heating a brand.

The pen was made of withies. Inside it half a dozen people stood linked arm to arm with rope. One groaned; another swore; a third wept; a fourth argued with someone who was not there. The fifth was Gifu.

She saw him. She rushed toward him; the rope caught her. "Bear," she cried. "Bear, they took my horse."

He drew his knife and cut her free. The three lawmen left the brand in the fire and strode toward him. One drew his sword. Bjarni took her by the hand and started toward the gate.

In loud French the three men challenged him, blocking his way. The man with the sword wore a coat of iron links over his shoulders. Bjarni stood a head taller than the tallest of them.

Gifu hugged his arm to her side. "They said I must have stolen the horse—tell them we got it honestly. Make them give me back my horse."

He looked around at the three men, ranged in a half-circle across his path. He clenched his fist. One by one their voices stilled, and their faces lengthened with doubt. The sword gleamed in the faint light from the fire. He stepped toward them, and the man with the sword backed away. One step behind, the others retreated after him. Bjarni led Gifu away around the tower.

Gifu nagged him to get her horse back. He kept her close by him, for fear she would be taken again. He had tired of Lincoln and thought of going on to London. He had been gone from home more than half the year. He dreamt of Hiyke, but in the dream he could not see her face, and Hoskuld stood behind her.

The king fell sick. He sent for Bjarni.

The tower was silent. The air had an unhealthy smell. In the king's bedchamber the king's friends stood solid against the walls. Red William lay propped on cushions, his hair combed over his shoulders. The cup in his hands was jeweled with rock crystal. He saw Bjarni above the heads of the others and summoned him to the bed.

The Norse priest was not there. The king lay back on his pillows and called in a fretful voice. His minions stirred and shifted their feet, and one came forward through the others, sliding by Bjarni to the king's side.

It was the man who dressed as a woman. Now he wore men's clothes, but his face was painted with red cheeks and lips and dark eyelashes. He spoke in English.

"The king is mysteriously sick. You have the gift—that is known. How may we break the curse?"

The king's blue eyes bulged; he looked gaunt. Bjarni looked him over, wondering if he were truly cursed. "He does not look fey to me," he said. Inside the collar of the king's nightshirt a string of hide encircled his neck. Bjarni reached down and lifted the string. He drew a piece of iron, a cross, and a clove of garlic out of the king's nightshirt.

Some of the men behind him gasped. The king caught hold of his hand.

Bjarni laughed. "Tell him he is sinking under the weight of his faith." He let Red William have the charms again, and the king stuck them away under his shirt. The high color tinged his face.

Bjarni said, "Tell him that he will not die in the straw.

That is marked all over him. Who can ask more than that?"

"His grace says you are impudent. He does not understand you. Make yourself plain."

The king looked angry. With his hand Bjarni saluted him and went out of the room.

THE KING WAS WELL AGAIN the next day. He called Bjarni into the tower and thanked him for destroying the curse.

"I did nothing," Bjarni said. "The king saved himself."

The king put a bag of money on the table before him. He said, "There is a ship at Grimsby to take you back to Iceland."

"Thank you," Bjarni said, surprised. "You are generous to me."

The king smiled at him. The Norse priest was translating for them. He said, "His grace says that you have asked nothing of him, and therefore he knows that you are to be trusted. He wishes you to make his name known in your country and to tell your friends and others of the power and the wealth of the King of England. Will you do so?"

That seemed easy enough, and Bjarni agreed to it. They were in the same small room where Bjarni had first spoken to Red William. Two little pages stood by. The king gestured to them, and they brought a beautiful long coat of velvet and lay it on Bjarni's shoulders, and they put on him a fancy belt and good boots. The king rose in his place. One of the pages brought him a sword.

"Kneel," said the king.

Bjarni said, "First tell me what this is all about."

"His grace will knight you and accept you into his service as his man."

Bjarni began to take off the coat. The king lowered the sword, his face ruddy. Bjarni said, "I am sorry to disappoint him, but I have never knelt down to anybody, except my father."

The king leaned on the sword. He shouted something at Bjarni, which the priest translated with a smile.

"You will have no ship. You will have to swim back to Iceland."

Bjarni shrugged. He slung the coat over the table, next to the bag of money.

The king's blazing blue eyes dimmed. He spoke sharply to a page, who went out. The priest knotted his fingers together. The king sat down again and fixed his gaze on Bjarni. There was a silence.

At last the king spoke. "His grace says that he should have expected this of you. Perhaps to a sorcerer wealth and power are so easy they mean nothing. Take the gifts. Take the ship. The word of such a man as you will have great weight in Iceland; he would rather be spoken of honestly by you than praised by a thousand sycophants."

Bjarni stood a moment, wondering what to say, and the remaining page brought the coat and helped him put it on again. The page who had gone returned with wine and cups. The king drank from a cup and passed it to Bjarni, who also drank, although he knew nothing of the rite. He thanked the king many times, took the bag of money, and left.

When he reached the inn again and went up the stairs, the door to his room was shut, and through it he heard two voices, Gifu's and a man's. Gifu was giggling. Bjarni went to the end of the corridor, where there was a window, and stood looking out over the thatches of the town. Eventually a strange man came out of the room behind him, doing the laces of his shirt.

Seeing Bjarni he stammered some words of French and hurried away to the stairs. Bjarni went into the room.

Gifu sat on the bed. Her skirt was bunched around her hips, and her long legs were bare. One hand rested on her rounding belly. She smiled at Bjarni.

"You slut," Bjarni said.

She held out her hand. Three pieces of silver lay on her palm. "Someone must keep us."

"The king keeps us."

"I like a pretty now and then." She fingered her money.

He took three ribbons from his sleeve and draped them over her shoulder. He had bought them for her in the market. She caught them up, crowing. "Bear. My favorite colors, too." She rushed around the room hunting for her looking glass. "Silly old Bear." She tied her red hair up in the blue ribbon.

Bjarni sat down on the bed. "I am going to Iceland. The king has found a ship for me."

She wheeled toward him, her face taut. Her eyes moved, taking in his new clothes. "Oh," she said. "What of me?"

"If you wish, you can go with me."

"I wish it."

"I am a farmer in Iceland, you know—it's a hard living. We work all day."

She leaned against his side and slid her arm around him. "I will work."

He thought of Hiyke and of his father. What would happen between them would follow in its own time. He was ready: more than ready.

"What will your family think of me?" Gifu asked.

"We will learn that when we get home," Bjarni said.

PART TWO

ḣIYKE AND HOSKULD slept together in the big carved bed he had built for his first wife. One night, when *Swan* had been gone more than a month, a sound woke Hiyke.

Hoskuld snored in the dark beside her. She climbed down from the bed and stood below the gutskin window in the ceiling.

"Who is there?"

"Mother," a voice whispered, through the window.

It was Kristjan's voice. She put her feet into her boots and pulled her shawl around her. Hoskuld slept on. She went out down the darkened hall to the door into the yard.

Soft snow was falling. Kristjan came to her and pulled her by the hand across the frozen yard toward the barn.

"Mother," he said, when they were inside the barn, and embraced her. One hand on his chest, she forced them apart.

"So you came back," she said. "Where are the rest?"

"In the ship," he said.

"And you want me to smooth things over for you with Hoskuld."

"Mother, he will heed you. Besides, it was all Bjarni's doing."

She was shivering. Her feet were cold. In the back of the barn a horse snuffled. She said, "Tell Bjarni himself to talk to Hoskuld," and turned back to the door.

"Bjarni is dead," Kristjan said.

That silenced her a moment. Presently, facing him again, she said, "What happened?"

"I am cold, Mother. That's a story for the hearth. Talk to Hoskuld for us."

"You good-for-nothing," she said. "You think so little of me." She spat off to his left. "I regret that I am your mother."

"Who is this?" Hoskuld said, behind her.

Barefoot, in his nightshirt, he came inside. He carried the axe in one hand.

"Oh," he said, and strode toward Kristjan. "It's your cub. Where are mine?"

She pulled Kristjan behind her. "They are nearby. I don't care what you do with them, but leave him alone."

"It was all Bjarni's idea," Kristjan said, over her shoulder. "We came back as soon as he was dead."

"Dead." Hoskuld lowered his hands. "You are sure? You saw him dead?"

"Not exactly—Sigurd took him. We stole Sigurd's daughter. Bjarni fell to them." Kristjan was leaning over Hiyke's shoulder to speak to his stepfather. His breath grazed her ear. "We came straight back, I swear it, as she is honest."

Hoskuld laughed. He took Hiyke by the hand and

nodded to Kristjan. "They can come back." He led her out through the snowy yard to the bedroom door. More than once he laughed.

THE GIRL WITH ULF was tall and fair. Her face was lovely. Hiyke sat beside Hoskuld in the High Seat; she saw how her husband looked at the girl.

"You are Sigurd's daughter," Hoskuld said. "You favor him. He was always a handsome man." He ignored his three sons, standing behind her. "Are you here of your own will?"

"Yes, my lord," the girl whispered.

"I am going to marry her," Ulf said.

"What is your name?" Hoskuld said.

"Gudrun, my lord."

Whenever she called him that, Hoskuld swelled. Hiyke sat unmoving in the seat beside him and kept silence.

"Well," he said, "I will give you the shelter of my hall, and for your sake, pretty Gudrun, I will take them back. Come here and sit by me. And now tell me your story."

Ulf stood between Jon on the left and Andres on the right. He said, "We found Sigurd's island and stayed there above ten days, but he and Bjarni could not agree. And he would not give me Gudrun. We left—we came back later and stole Gudrun while they were all in the church, but they caught Bjarni. We barely escaped ourselves. Sigurd had hundreds of men there."

Hoskuld smiled. He had forgotten Gudrun at his side; he looked only at Ulf. He said, "I meant Sigurd to do away with him. I thought he had outrun me when he left me behind. But you did my work for me. Fate's work, it was; that is clear."

Andres said, "We did not wish his death—we did not cause his death."

Beside him, Ulf looked down at his feet.

"You did," Hoskuld said. "Don't tell me otherwise. Haul *Swan* up onto the beach. We have hay to mow."

Gudrun would not marry Ulf until he took Christ. She slept on a pallet in the little room in the back of the hall where Hiyke and Hoskuld slept. Ulf never saw her alone; Hoskuld managed that. She spent the day washing her face and hands and putting clothes on. Ulf tried to talk her into marrying him as he was, but she refused. She fawned on Hoskuld. She had a pretty, shy, mild way about her that seemed false to Hiyke.

The days grew short. They brought in the yearling sheep to be slaughtered. Hoskuld kept them all hard at the work, except Kristjan, who did as little as he could. One night when they were in their bedchamber Hoskuld said, "That is a lazy, weakling brat you have."

Gudrun was sitting on her pallet in the corner, listening. Hiyke motioned at her with her head, to remind Hoskuld. She did not want to argue with him in front of her.

The man pushed her. "Did you hear me? I said that I will hasten him out of here unless he works."

She burned at that. "If he goes, I will go," she said.

"Go, then!" He leaned over her, shouting into her ear, as he always did. "Go beg on the road. That's all he is worth. That, and drowning."

Gudrun was watching all this intently, a smile on her lips. Hiyke bit her lips to keep from swearing at him. He roared at her; he was half-drunk. He tramped out of the room and across the hall to the High Seat, and Hiyke heard him bellow for his jug.

Her hands shook. She wished that she had struck him, to take the edge off her anger. Between her and Gudrun there passed an instant's glance. Gudrun lowered her head over the looking glass in her lap. Hiyke went out to the hall.

Hoskuld sat there in the High Seat. The pelt of a black bear hid the pagan carvings on the back. His shaggy fair hair stood out against the glossy fur. She went down the hall to the door.

Kristjan was sitting in the grass behind the shed, playing on a little flute of bone. She took the flute from him and broke it in her hands.

"You are a disgrace to me," she said. "For my sake he tolerates it, but I will not. Either you work or you go."

Kristjan raised his dark frowning face toward her. "Why should I work for him? I hate him. I hate them all."

"Then do it for me," she said.

He caught her hand and kissed the palm. "I will," he said. Getting to his feet, he put his arms around her; he was only slightly taller than she was. She put her head down a moment on his shoulder.

SHE RODE along the beach, looking for shells. As she rode she thought that she might leave Hoskuld. Even while she considered it, her mind resisted it.

Her first two years at Hrafnfell had been hard ones. The fish had disappeared out of the sea and half the lambs had died. She had worked beside Hoskuld and his sons until she could not walk. She had climbed up the cliff after eggs and gathered seaweed and boiled it for soup. Now the life here was better. She had earned her life here, and she would not give it up.

The grey mare picked her way over the rocky beach. Hiyke kept watch for the small shells that she used to dye her wool. Her hands were cold. She reined the mare down toward the sea. Now she did not look for shells; she stared out to sea.

Married at fifteen, she lost her husband to the sea barely a year later, when Kristjan was still unnoticed in her womb. For twelve years she had lived with her husband's family, carding the wool, spinning and weaving, as a good Christian woman did. Her husband's family was well-born, their house stocked with servants. Hiyke did no harsh work. Yet she longed for work, for the test. Then one day she had seen a blond-haired man at the gate who stood a head taller than anyone else on the farm.

It was a sin, to love Hoskuld. Yet she paid her penance, every day, hauling water and scrubbing the floor, and bearing Hoskuld himself. She crossed herself, sure that

God understood her. The grey sea churned the surf around her horse's feet. She urged the mare on, looking for shells.

WHEN HOSKULD HAD SLAUGHTERED the yearling lambs he culled the weanlings and took the finest of them and washed it. He made his yearly joke about giving a gelded sheep to the god of his manhood. This he did before everyone, not caring that it was against the law.

"Who will go with me?" he said. "Kristjan?"

Kristjan said nothing.

"Jon? Andres?"

"No, Papa."

"Ulf?"

Ulf turned away. Hoskuld pulled back his lip in a smile. "Cross-kisser," he said. He took the lamb over his shoulders and the axe in his hand and went up the hillside, toward the great bulging rock of the Raven Cliff.

Hiyke and Gudrun were watching from the side of the yard. Gudrun turned to her. "Where is he going?"

"To sacrifice," Hiyke said. "He gives the lamb to his demon, Thor."

Ulf was coming toward them. Gudrun held out her hands to him. "You did not go," she said, and went into his arms.

. . .

ULF AND GUDRUN were married by Eirik Arnarson's priest, in the church at the chieftain's farm. They knelt down together to take the Body of Christ. Afterward the wedding party sailed across the bay to Hrafnfell to feast the couple. Hoskuld gave his son a fur cloak. He gave Gudrun a necklace of gold links. She laughed, thanking him, and kissed him.

"Be careful," Hiyke said, when the bride had left them. "She might confuse herself over the bridegroom."

"She might be the fatter for it," he said. He lifted the jug.

"Not from you, Hoskuld."

They were sitting together in the High Seat. Up and down the hall, the guests and the people of Hrafnfell were dancing. Even Eirik Arnarson had joined them.

"It is not my misdoing you do not bear," he said to her. He pushed the jug at her. "Drink."

She stuck her chin up. He leaned toward her and said into her ear, "What, do you not trust yourself with it?"

Taking the jug, she lifted it and drank of the mead. He laughed at her.

"Here comes Eirik Arnarson," she said. "If I were you, I would turn sober before you make a fool of yourself."

Hoskuld put the jug down. The chieftain came to the opposite side of the table, and they shook hands. The table was between them; Hiyke had heard that was a bad omen.

"There is no more word of Bjarni?" Eirik asked, when they had done with the amenities.

"Nothing," said Hoskuld.

"That is much to our loss, here," Eirik said. "Much to our loss." Standing straight and fat and soft before Hoskuld, he said, "Even worse are these rumors about it. I would take it ill if you brought about what happened to your son, Hoskuld."

Hoskuld gave a careless laugh. "What, little man, would you fight with me over it?" He gestured to Hiyke. "She will tell you I am innocent. Tell him, woman." Heaving himself out of the double chair, he went away down the room.

Eirik looked at her, blinking. His small mouth was tucked down at the corners.

"He did nothing," she said, which was true.

"Damn him," Eirik said.

"This is our hall," she said, sharply. "And you would not curse him to his face, would you." She went away from him. A few steps away, she glanced over her shoulder. Eirik stood there facing the empty High Seat. His mouth worked in and out. Swallowing the insults. There was no justice in him, not for Hoskuld or for anyone else. She crossed the hall, her throat dry, to find some drink.

Near the wall she came abruptly face to face with Eirik's priest. When she would have gone by him the priest stepped into her path.

"Hiyke Ragnarsdottir, I would be pleased to see you at Mass."

"I have better things to do," she said, "than spend half a day listening to you misinterpret the Scriptures."

She had gone once to his church, and he had chosen as his text for the sermon the words of Saint Paul that it was better to marry than to burn. Since then she had prayed by herself.

The priest picked at his nose. His eyes burned with zeal. He said, "Remember the parable of the strayed sheep, my daughter."

"I will find my own way to God," she said. "Let me by."

"Your way. That is your sin, Hiyke Ragnarsdottir, to prefer your own way over God's way."

As he warmed to his lecture he waggled his finger and his voice swelled, and the people around them turned to look and listen. Hiyke brushed by the priest. She felt the eyes on her like venom in the air. She got a cupful of mead and drank deep to steady herself.

She drank much that day. Night fell, and she was as drunken as the rest. The wedding couple were put to bed in the sleeping booth. In the yard the guests danced and drank by the light of torches. Hiyke's head was pounding, and her stomach churned. The light dazzled her eyes. The murky shapes of the dancers whirled before her.

A great goat danced before her. The horns curved back from its round brow. Hoskuld danced with the goat. He lumbered in a circle and the goat stood on its hind legs and drove its horned head at him.

The guests screamed, laughing; all the sound mixed together in her ears. Her tongue flicked over her lips. Her gaze was fixed on Hoskuld. He led the goat around again in their clumsy dance. The goat reared and put its hoofs on his chest. Reaching down, crouching, he caressed the beast's balls with his hands. The goat bleated, and Hiyke stirred, her thighs warm. The wild shadows of the goat and the man lapped against the sleeping booth, where Ulf and Gudrun shared the wedding bed.

Hoskuld drove the goat away. He came toward Hiyke, bringing the scent of the beast. He spread out his hands for her to see. On his palms he had drawn the runes of her name. She trembled from head to foot. She coiled her arms around his neck, and their mouths met, and their bodies pressed together. He took her away down the hall to their bed.

HOSKULD AND ULF played chess, and Hoskuld won. After that he would not play with Ulf again.

"You are no challenge. I am used to opponents who know the game."

Ulf flushed. "Let me try. Once more."

"Bjarni would never have been trapped that easily," Hoskuld said. "He never made mistakes."

"He made one," Ulf said. "Or he would not be dead now."

"He is dead because you are a coward and a weakling," Hoskuld said.

Hiyke was watching this from behind her loom. Gudrun sat on the hearth; she watched also. Ulf stood to face his father. His face was dark with temper. His fists knotted.

"Do not fight in the hall," Hiyke said. She threaded her shuttle with the grey wool.

"He will not fight," Hoskuld said. "Because it is the truth."

"Come outside," Ulf said.

Hoskuld was placing the chesspieces back at the edges of the board. "Sit down," he said.

"Come outside!"

Hoskuld got up from the High Seat. The bear fur was matted where he had been. Ulf went ahead of him toward the door. Before he reached the step, Hoskuld sprang on him from behind and struck him down.

Gudrun screamed. Hiyke stood, dropping the shuttle. The weights on her loom clinked together.

Hoskuld spoke to Ulf, lying at his feet. "Your brother was worth ten of you. He would never have trusted me behind him." He came back to the High Seat.

Ulf rose. He swayed, half-dazed by the blow. Hoskuld beckoned to Hiyke.

"Come. I will teach you the game."

Hiyke put away her yarns. Ulf was staring at his father, but his arms hung at his sides, and he did not challenge Hoskuld again. He went to the door. On the steps he stumbled and nearly fell. Gudrun followed him out of the hall.

Andres, Jon, and Kristjan were still sitting at the table. Hiyke took her place in the High Seat. Hoskuld turned the chessboard so that it was between them. His sons and his stepson watched him without looking away.

"You are all as shameful as Ulf," Hoskuld said. "You all killed Bjarni."

Jon lowered his eyes. Beside him, Kristjan put his feet outside the bench and walked out of the hall, and no one called him back. Hoskuld was bent over the chessboard, but all his attention lay on his sons.

"Tell me again how you left him behind to die."

"Hoskuld," Hiyke said. "That is between them and God."

"Keep quiet," he said.

Andres stood, his hands on the table bracing him. "If Bjarni is dead, then by his way of thinking he died well, and if he is not dead, then we are guilty of nothing. I am going to sleep." He too left the hall.

Hoskuld said, "That is a mouse-minded thought." His shadow lay broad across the table. Only Jon faced him now, his cheeks sucked thin, and his mouth tight.

"Tell me how you left him," Hoskuld said.

Jon swallowed. Slowly he began to tell that story, already old. Hiyke studied the chessboard before her. She knew the actions of the pieces. She shut her ears to Jon's voice.

IN THE RAIN of an autumn storm Hiyke rode around the end of the bay to a nearby farm, to help a woman there bear a baby. Several other women of the farms around the bay had also come. They brought forth the baby in its time and Hiyke washed it and swaddled it; the other women went about neatening the room and making the mother comfortable. It was a small, mean hut with only one room, and the man too lazy even to make lamps. He sat in the corner by the hearth drinking birch tea as the women tended his wife and child.

Hiyke took the baby to its mother. The woman lay like an emptied sack on the bed; she looked on the baby without love. Hiyke slid it into the curve of its mother's arm.

"Ah, well," the woman said. "One more won't make such a difference."

Her older children were all outdoors, even in the rain. Hiyke got a broom and swept the hearth.

Later the woman called her over to the bedside again. She took Hiyke's fingers in her moist hand.

"Hiyke," she said. "You are well off, there at Hrafnfell. We are so poor, and my children are sick. Please, can you give us something to keep us through the winter?"

Hiyke glanced up at the other women, all watching her. Her neck and cheeks began to heat unpleasantly. She said, "I shall ask Hoskuld to give your man a place on *Swan.*"

The woman in the bed let go of her hand. "Our stomachs won't wait until the fishing begins." She lifted the newborn in her arms for Hiyke to look at. "We'll all starve."

One of the other women said, "For Christian mercy, Hiyke Ragnarsdottir—everyone knows how your storerooms bulge at Hrafnfell."

"Because we work," Hiyke said. "Because we care for ourselves."

Their faces were shut against her. One said, "Mysterious it is, why God exalts some people, in spite of their sins."

"For Christ's sweet sake," another said, "Hiyke Ragnarsdottir, have you no reason to crave Christ's mercy? Think, now."

They stood there talking about sin to her, talking about mercy, while in the corner by the hearth the man drank tea she had brewed.

"I shall ask Hoskuld to make a place for him on *Swan,* when he goes fishing again." She nodded to the other women. "And now I will go."

She went out slowly, so that they would not think she was running away. The grey mare was tethered in the lee of the hut. The oldest child had brought it some grass in his hand and stood feeding it. Seeing her, he stepped back hastily to let her by. His face was pale. He watched her with awe. She knew that the women called her witch-names behind her back; the children heard it, made it into songs, which they sang in her hearing. She swung her leg and her skirt up across the saddle and turned the mare's head toward Hrafnfell.

The rain had stopped. Round clouds still covered the sky. She rode at a gallop along the green slope. On her left the dark mountain stood; on her right was the head of the bay, the waves softened to little curls of foam. She rode to the stream that came down the mountainside from the glacier.

Someone sat on a stone on the far side. She reined in.

It was Kristjan; he stood up and crossed the broad, shallow stream toward her. The water was smoky from the glacier. It piled up against his legs as he waded through it.

"What are you doing out here in the rain?" she asked. Her temper was still mean.

"The rain has stopped," Kristjan said.

She put the mare at the stream but it refused. Kristjan took the bridle and together they urged the horse to cross the water. Hiyke looked up into the sky. The clouds were parting. She saw blue through the grey.

She said, "These people have no idea of justice."

Kristjan raised his head, turning his dark eyes on her. "What happened?"

"Ah, they begged."

He led the mare onto the dry land, and she took him up behind her. The mare started off at a trot. Ahead the trail wound up the slope toward the pass through the mountains. The ditch was full of hawkweed. The sheep had clipped the grass on the far side almost to the ground.

"There is no value in justice if God will forgive all sins anyway," she burst out. "We eat because we work—if we feed all the lazy people through the good years, when the bad years come, we shall all starve and die."

Kristjan said, "Do what you will, Mama."

It rankled like a thorn under the skin that the other women should have spoken so to her. She urged the mare into a flying gallop toward the walls of Hrafnfell.

. . .

THE NIGHTS LENGTHENED into winter. Rain and snow fell. The earth shook several times a day for a few days. When the rain paused, Hiyke saddled the grey mare again and rode over the hill, to make certain that the springs where the sheep watered were still sweet to drink. On the way, Hoskuld and another man came into sight ahead of her, moving fast along the path toward her.

The other man was Jon. He walked hunched over like a crone; she did not recognize him until he was close. Hoskuld's lips were moving. He talked steadily to his son, who hurried on ahead as if he could outrun what Hoskuld said. Hiyke reined in the horse.

Jon passed her without a word. She pulled the mare around to block Hoskuld's way.

"Did you taste the water at Grim's Meadow?"

"Yes, yes," he said.

Jon was disappearing over the top of the hill. She said, "Why are you doing this? Why are you ripping at them over Bjarni?"

"He was my son," Hoskuld said. "Who else but I should avenge him?" He struck the mare on the flank, and she shied away. He walked past her, after Jon.

IN THE LONG NIGHT Hiyke kneaded her bread by the deep yellow light of a soapstone lamp. The wind slowed her way to the barn and helped her along on the way back. The men sat in the hall drinking and playing chess.

Andres read to them. Hiyke worked at her loom. No one made poems.

Hoskuld suddenly stood up from the High Seat and staggered a step and fell headlong.

Hiyke threw down her work and knelt by him. He was breathing. He stank of drink. At first she thought he was only drunk, and she made Ulf and Jon carry him to his bed.

She sat there in the flickering light of the lamp and said her prayers. The storm boomed and flapped against the gutskin window over her head.

"Stop muttering your female curses," Hoskuld whispered, "and bring me the jug."

"You don't need any more of the jug."

He heaved himself out of the bed and tramped through the door to the hall. Hiyke followed after him. Standing on the threshold he staggered a little and caught himself again.

His three sons and her son had put their heads together across the table. They watched Hoskuld enter; their eyes glittered. He crossed through the yellow light of the hearth and picked the jug off the table. When he turned to go, the four younger men set on him.

Hoskuld went down. Hiyke seized the heavy fire-iron. Swinging it full around her she beat them away from him. She stood over him, protecting him; Ulf and Jon and Andres crouched before her, their fingers hooked and their faces twisted into snarls. Kristjan backed away from them. By the table, Gudrun watched with shining eyes.

Hoskuld tried to stand. Hiyke caught his arm; she braced him up, his great weight pressing on her shoulder.

"Come to bed," she said.

He resisted her. Unsteadily he moved forward down the hall. With the fire-iron in her hand she guarded him, and he rounded the table and sat in the High Seat.

His eyes closed. Frightened, she wheeled around, shielding him from the others. "Get out!" She brandished the fire-iron at them, and they fled her, all but Gudrun, who stayed where she was.

"Go with them," Hiyke said to her.

The fair girl raised her eyes, wide and clear as glass. She said, "Poor Hoskuld," and laughed. At her leisure, she went out of the hall.

"Those dogs," Hoskuld said.

She sat beside him, wondering how she would get him to the safety of his bed. He put his hand to his chest.

"It hurts here." He sounded puzzled.

She realized now that it was more than the night's drinking. She clasped her hands together. "Holy Father," she said, and knew she could ask for nothing.

"Hiyke," he said, "stop mumbling."

"Can you walk?"

He pushed himself onto his feet. "I am just drunk." His cold fingers gripped her hand. "Come to bed, wife." His feet dragged over the floor. She helped him; it seemed to take the whole winter night, that traveling to their marriage bed.

. . .

HOSKULD DID NOT RISE. He kept the jug by his bed. Hiyke would not fill it, yet it was always full.

Once she came into the bedroom and found Gudrun there, sitting on the foot of the bed.

"The poor man, someone must keep him company," she said. She slid down to the floor and went out of the room, past Hiyke in the doorway. Hoskuld snored full-throated in the bed, the jug under his hand.

After that she sat in the room with him whenever he was awake. When he was cold, she brought him blankets, but then he complained that he was too hot.

"I am dying like a woman," he said. "Bjarni had the better death."

She lay down on the bed beside him and held his hand. "You need not die."

"I am dying."

"Say only, *I believe in God,* and you will not really die."

He turned away his head, groaning.

She tried to pray but it was as if a wall rose between her and God. For hours she crouched on her knees on the floor by the bed, wordless and hopeless. From one such false prayer she rose to find him unconscious in the bed. She went to the cookhouse and there in the warmth covered her face with her shawl and wept.

Gudrun found her there. "Well, Hiyke," she said, "you are a river of tears lately."

Hiyke thrust her shawl back. She turned to the cupboard and snapped open the doors.

Behind her, Gudrun said, "You have never taken any

pleasure or joy of life; I do not wonder Hoskuld is dying of it."

Hiyke wheeled around on her and slapped her. Gudrun stepped back. Her pale eyes narrowed like a snake's.

"You will pay for that," she said. She went out of the cookhouse. Hiyke rubbed her stinging palm on her skirt.

HOSKULD WOKE AGAIN. He seemed a little better. He called them all into the room and sat up and told them his will for the inheritance of his goods.

He gave the farm to Ulf, with *Swan* and the stock and the fishing rights and wood-cutting rights. To Jon and Andres he gave ten marks each, and he paid it out to them there, stacking the silver money on the bedcover before them. To Kristjan he gave five marks.

"You may stay here as long as you wish," he said to Hiyke. "You may live here forever if you wish. We had differences, but in all my life no other woman suited me as well as you."

She could not answer him. With Kristjan's silver in her fist she stood at the side of the bed, her dry eyes burning. He lay down again.

"As for Bjarni, I leave him nothing."

"Bjarni is dead," Ulf said.

"You did not see him die," Hoskuld said. "He will come back. I came back."

He shut his eyes. When he began to snore, they left him there with Hiyke.

Hoskuld died there, in the dark. On hearing it, Ulf and his brothers cheered and shouted like fools in a game. Kristjan dug the grave. The ground was soaked from the rains and the pit filled rapidly with water. None of Hoskuld's children came to bury him. Hiyke knelt down in the mud and prayed, but the prayers were for herself, not for Hoskuld. Kristjan stood behind her. When she could not pray anymore, she fell to weeping, and he lifted her. With his arms around her, he turned her away from the grave. He stroked her cheek. For the last time she wept for Walking Hoskuld.

GUDRUN CAME TO HER, a few days later, and said, "Now that Hoskuld is dead, I suppose you will go home to your family."

Hiyke put her feet on the rails of the loom. The cloth filled the top third of it, light grey, with the double black stripe up the side she used on all her goods.

"You heard Hoskuld," she said. "I shall stay at Hrafnfell."

"If you wish," Gudrun said. "But you cannot sleep where you are. That is the finest bed at Hrafnfell, and I mean to have it."

"It is my bed!"

Kristjan was by the hearth, watching. He came closer to listen.

Gudrun said, "I am mistress here now, Hiyke."

Hiyke did not answer that.

"I shall speak to Ulf," Gudrun said, and made as if to go. Hiyke caught her arm.

"I have no wish to be humiliated. I will sleep in the loft in the barn."

Gudrun put her head to one side, smiling. "You may have the small clothes-chest."

Kristjan came past her to his mother. "I will help you take your things to the loft," he said.

They gathered the sheets and the featherbed she had brought with her from her husband's home, packed her clothes, and took them through the yard to the barn. The loft was half full of straw. She spread out some and laid her bed on it.

"Perhaps we should go," Kristjan said. "My father's brother will take us in again."

She picked straw from her hair. "I will be here when she is wormridden," she said. Her voice trembled. "I swear it. I swear it."

PART THREE

Climbing toward the pass through the mountains, Bjarni came into the sunshine, and he paused there, in the light. Gifu huffed and groaned up the steep trail behind him. After the weeks at sea she was soft and easily tired. Waiting, he lifted his gaze to the black peaks all around him. The wind keened off the serried edges of the rocks. He went on a few steps.

"Wait!" she cried, still many yards below him.

"I am waiting."

He had moved only to widen his view to the east, through the gap between the lava blades of the mountains, to where the sun burned on the glacier. Panting, Gifu reached his side.

"Shall I carry you?" he said.

"No—" She came gratefully to a halt. Her hand rested on the curve of her belly. "How far now?"

"Just a little farther on."

"You said that an hour ago."

"We are close now." He nodded up to the summit of the pass, where the trail ran through a notch in the stony slopes. "That is the top. It's easier walking downhill."

She started off again. Bjarni went along beside her. He

carried both their bundles on his shoulder. They climbed past rocks spotted with lichens. In the joints of the stone, coarse yellow flowers grew. They reached the summit, and the path turned down.

He held himself to Gifu's pace, although he longed to go on at top speed. A fold of the hillside shut him in against the mountain. The downward slope pulled him faster, and he slowed his feet. Gifu breathed harshly beside him. The path ran out along the bare side of the hill, and the whole valley opened up to his view.

He stopped. There was his home before him, the long narrow bay, the faceted water winking in the sun, and on the left the sheer face of the Raven Cliff. Sheep trails crisscrossed the slope below it. The buildings were small and low in the grass.

He started down the path and stopped again. Midway between him and the bottom of the path was a little dale where birch trees grew. The wind had bowed the trees and turned their branches all to one side. A woman was walking through the trees toward the path.

At the edge of the path, she saw Bjarni and Gifu above her. She paused. It was Hiyke.

She recognized him; she dropped the bundle in her hands and stood staring at him. He went down the hillside toward her, leaving Gifu behind.

He said, "Well met, Hiyke."

Hiyke stooped to gather up the bundle. She had been carrying pieces of birch bark in her black shawl, and the bark had scattered over the ground at her feet. She collected everything into the shawl again. Straightening, the bundle tight in her fists, she came a step toward Bjarni.

"Bjarni," she said. "It is you. So you have come back. Hoskuld said that you would."

"Did he say what I would do to him, when I was here?"

She said, "Hoskuld is dead."

"Dead. Of what cause?"

"He died of drink," she said. "Last winter. In the long night."

He noticed now that all her clothes were black. Fine lines webbed the corners of her eyes. She looked weathered and hard. He could hear Gifu coming down the path behind him, and Hiyke was watching her, intent. She lifted her thin black brows at him.

"Where have you been? It was nearly a year ago that you sailed away."

"In England," he said.

Gifu trudged the last few steps to his side and slid her hand under his arm and leaned on his side.

Hiyke said, "Is this your wife?"

"No. She is not my wife, the child is not mine."

"Well, come home," Hiyke said. "You must be tired."

They started on again. Gifu walked between them. Bjarni told her Hiyke's name, and told her name to Hiyke. They walked a little way in silence. Bjarni thought of his father. He had leaned on his hate of Hoskuld; the death unsettled him.

Hiyke said, "That is a beautiful coat you are wearing, Bjarni."

"The King of England gave it to me."

"And the gold belt?"

"Yes, that too."

Hiyke wagged her head a little. "All this while, we have thought you were dead."

They were coming toward Hrafnfell. The high grass rose and fell like waves of the sea; the sod roofs of the buildings stirred like the rest. Gifu clung to his arm. Hiyke went ahead of them toward the farmhouse.

Ulf was in the yard, saddling the grey mare. Bent to reach for the girth, he did not see Bjarni until he was almost on him. He wheeled. All the color fled out of his face, and he clenched his fist in the mane of the mare.

"Bjarni."

Bjarni put out his hand. "Welcome me back, brother."

"I welcome you," Ulf said. He gripped Bjarni's hand hard. "Well—well—you are welcome." He pumped Bjarni's hand up and down.

"Who is that?"

Bjarni turned and raised his head. Kristjan stood before the barn. He saw who Bjarni was, and he yelled. His hand flew up to cross himself. Andres came out of the barn behind him.

"Bjarni." Widely he smiled, his two hands out. He brushed past Kristjan. "Bjarni. Where did you come from? Who is this?" He nodded to Gifu; he set his hands on Bjarni's arms, smiling.

"Come inside," Ulf said to Bjarni. "You look as if you've traveled far."

Bjarni put his hand on Gifu's shoulder. "She is tired. Let me show her where she can rest."

Ulf had put a stiff smile on his face. "Yes—naturally—"

"I'm hungry," Gifu said.

Hiyke reached for her hand. "Come with me. You can rest in my bed." She paid Bjarni's coat and belt another look and took Gifu away.

Bjarni followed Ulf into the hall. The room was hot from the buried fire in the hearth. Ulf walked one step ahead of him toward the High Seat.

A woman sat in it. The black bear fur set off her pale beauty.

"See who has come back," Ulf said to her. He swung his hand toward Bjarni.

Gudrun's face did not change. For a moment, her gaze on Bjarni, she said nothing. Finally she turned to Ulf.

"Is the horse ready?" she said.

"Yes."

She stooped for the red cloak on the bench by her feet. She said, "Welcome to our home, Bjarni Hoskuldsson." The red cloak went around her shoulders, and she came down from the High Seat toward Ulf. "Now I am going to hear Mass. Are you coming, husband?"

Bjarni fingered the gold rings of the buckle of his belt. Ulf hesitated. At the steps up to the door, his wife waited for him. He clapped Bjarni on the shoulder. "I will be back. You must be tired. Rest and eat." He followed Gudrun out to the yard.

Bjarni set down the bundles he carried on his shoulder.

He took off his belt and coat and went to the fire. He looked
long around him. The High Seat stood out crooked from
the table as if Hoskuld had just left it. A lamp lay to the
side of the hearth; its string had broken. The door creaked
open, and Andres came in and walked down the room toward Bjarni. Kristjan trailed after him.

"Where did you go?" Andres said. "How did you get
back?"

"Do you mean, how did I escape from Sigurd?" He sat
down on the stones of the hearth. "With no help from
you."

Andres rubbed his hands together. "We were afraid. We
could not make up our minds what to do—you always
decided what we should do. So we came back home."

"There was nothing we could do," Kristjan said. "There
were too many of them to fight. We thought they would
kill you straightaway."

"Spoken like an Irishman," Bjarni said.

Andres pulled the end of the bench out and sat on it,
facing him. "That's true. It was our fault. As for me, I want
your forgiveness."

"That's a Christian word," Bjarni said. He got up and
walked around the hall, looking at the familiar things.

"Is that girl your wife?" Andres said.

"No. She is an English girl. Her family saved my life
when I was running away from Sigurd."

"God bless her for that, then," Andres said.

Kristjan snorted; he went out of the hall. Bjarni said,
"Stop, Andres."

His half brother began to speak, indignant. Bjarni followed Kristjan out to the yard.

Hiyke met him halfway to the cookhouse.

"Gifu is asleep," she said. "In the loft."

"The loft?"

"That is where I sleep now, since Gudrun wanted the marriage bed."

They went down into the cookhouse. On the stone table there were crocks of milk set out to separate. Bjarni sat down. Hiyke put fish and bread and a piece of cheese on the table at his elbow.

"Gudrun went on to the church," Hiyke said.

He nodded. The cookhouse was too dark to see her face distinctly. The bread was fresh and he ate it all. She went around the cookhouse, wrapping the rest of the cheese and putting it on the shelf.

"You must wonder at your welcome," she said.

"They thought I was dead."

"They thought that they had killed you."

He had expected a worse welcome, and yet a better one, with everything solved in one blow. He said, "I am alive, you see."

"Yes—she told me how." Hiyke faced him again, closer. The light lay on her cheek. Her eyes were clear blue. "Such things are heard of in tales, mostly."

"She lies. Don't put weight on anything she says." He took his English dagger to cut the piece of cheese. "I am not here to satisfy myself with Ulf and the others. Is that what they are afraid of?"

"Yes, I think so."

"I am not."

"That is an excellent knife."

"The King of England gave it to me," he said.

"Oh. Then she does not lie all the time?"

He put out his hand and took hold of her skirt. She stepped back. He let her go. With a sweep of her hand she pulled her skirt back out of his reach.

He said, "You know why I left. For that reason I came back."

The shadow veiled her face again. She said, "I am in no mood for amorous talk."

The door flew open, and Jon came down into the cookhouse. He had not seen Bjarni. He passed Hiyke, pulling off his coat in the warmth of the oven, and then saw Bjarni sitting there against the wall.

Jon's eyes popped. He stammered out, "Papa."

Bjarni got to his feet. He tipped his head forward to keep from striking the roofbeams.

"Why did you come back?" Jon shouted. "Why didn't you stay where you belong? Why did you come back?" He burst up the steps and out the door. Hiyke watched him go.

Bjarni sat down again. He passed his hand over his face.

The door hung halfway open. Hiyke went to the second step and pushed it shut. She turned toward Bjarni again. Her eyes were wide and bright.

"He tormented them, Hoskuld. He shamed them for deserting you. So there is that in their greeting of you."

"I have no interest in that," he said. "I am here for your sake."

"Bah," she said, and looked angry. "You are here for your own sake, to have me. It is not so easy as that—just to want."

"Ah, Hiyke," he said.

Her face was grimly set. She stared at him a moment, went up the step, and opened the door, letting in the dusty sunlight as she left.

BJARNI SLEPT in the sleeping booth, in the bed against the hillside. In the night he went out behind the booth to piss. On his way back to the door, he saw Jon creep into the booth ahead of him, hunched over like an old man. Bjarni watched him from the door. The banked fire in the hearth gave enough light to see by.

Jon stole across the room, going from one bed to the next. At each he looked to see who lay there. In the first he found Kristjan, and in the second he found Andres. On the foot of the third bed he found the fine velvet coat that King William had given Bjarni. With the coat was the English dagger.

Jon drew the dagger out of its sheath. He lifted it in both hands and plunged it down into the bearskin under which Bjarni had been lying. His arms pumped up and down half a dozen times with the dagger.

Behind him, Bjarni said, "Am I dead yet?"

Jon screamed. He dropped the dagger. He spun around. Only a few feet separated him from Bjarni. He screamed again and dashed across the booth to the door.

Andres called out, "What is it?" Kristjan was standing in the dark at the foot of his bed, the blanket around him, and his knife in his hand.

Bjarni said, "Maybe he thought I was having trouble sleeping." He took the dagger out of the rent bearskin. He did not go to bed again.

When he went to the hall for his breakfast, Ulf and Gudrun were still away at the Christian church. He sat down over a dish of lamb and duck's eggs. Kristjan came to him.

"Jon sent me here," Hiyke's son said, without preliminary.

Bjarni nodded, chewing his meat.

"He did not intend it," Kristjan said. "He was overwrought. It was old Hoskuld he struck at, not you."

Bjarni lifted his head. Sitting down, he was at eye level with Kristjan. The boy was fifteen; he would always be puny, dark as a dwarf. Bjarni said, "You are still the go-between."

"Yes," Kristjan said.

"I will not ruin your luck. Go tell Jon that I have forgotten what he did."

The dark youth went away. Bjarni crossed the yard to the loft, to see how Gifu was.

Hiyke was gone. Gifu sat cross-legged on the straw bed, taking clothes from her pack.

"This is such a strange place—the night seems only an hour long." Gifu stood to put on her dress. The bulge of her growing baby thrust out her shift.

Later in the day Bjarni went to the hall again and found

Ulf there, sitting in the High Seat with Gudrun beside him. Ulf rose to his feet to greet him. They shook hands and Bjarni sat down on the bench beside his brother.

"I am glad to see you," Ulf said. "Hiyke said that you made your fortune in England. I am surprised you came back. I am glad, too," he added hastily.

Bjarni looked past him at Gudrun, sitting in the High Seat, her hands in her lap. He shortened his gaze to Ulf again. "Of course I came back. What happened to Hoskuld?"

"Don't believe what Hiyke tells you. He drank himself to death."

Bjarni laid his forearms on the table. "That she told me." He laced his fingers together. "What happened back at Sigurd's holm?"

His brother fingered his jaw. Beside him, Gudrun leaned forward and spoke in her cool voice. "Be plain with him, husband."

"Hoskuld intended Sigurd to kill you," Ulf said. "We thought you were dead, there, on the beach."

"My father surely did not set you free," Gudrun said.

"No. I escaped from him." He nodded to Ulf. "I will be as plain as that with you, brother. Hoskuld is dead, and I his eldest son, but you have his place in the High Seat."

"He disinherited you," Ulf said. "He left you nothing."

Bjarni sat back. Gudrun was smiling. She said, "You are welcome here, Bjarni Hoskuldsson, as long as you wish to stay."

He left them there, sitting together in the High Seat. He went out of the hall and across the hillside. The wind chilled his burning face. He strode along the slope, not caring where he went, until his eye caught on the graveyard, higher on the hill. He walked up to it. Within the fence of chunks of lava were two rows of graves. None of the humps was marked, but by the fresh soft grass he knew which was Hoskuld's. He spat on that grave.

He stood there deep in black thoughts. The sound of a horse coming brought him back to himself. Hiyke, on the bay gelding, was galloping down from the height below the cliff.

He stepped back from the graveyard. She drew rein above him and crossed her hands over the saddlebow.

"What are you doing there? You can't reach him now; you are wasting your curses."

Bjarni walked through knee-high grass to her side. "Why can I not reach him—he reached me from beyond the grave —he fed me ashes this day."

They went along the slope toward the hall. On the cliff above them the ravens clamored. Their shadows swept over the grass. Below, near the shore of the bay, *Swan* rode on her reflection in the quiet water. He returned his gaze to Hiyke, riding beside him. He let his eyes feed on her. She gripped the rein in her two hands. Today she seemed no older than a girl. Her face was sunbrowned, her mouth ripely curved. Suddenly she reined in.

"It is your farm," she said. "You should have it. Ulf has let all the work go. You see how the place is kept. They neither fish nor mow nor shear the sheep, without someone to tell them."

"We will go to the Althing soon," he said. "I will talk to Eirik Arnarson and the other chiefs and see if Hoskuld's will cannot be set aside."

"Talk? I cannot understand you. How can you come back and find what you find and simply talk?"

He took the rein and made the bay horse turn, so that he and Hiyke were face to face. "I told you why I came back here," he said.

She lifted the rein in her hands. "Take Hrafnfell," she said. Her eyes glittered. "Take the High Seat, and I will give you what you desire of me. Now free me."

He opened his fingers. She galloped the horse away down the hill. He stood in the grass. The shadows of the ravens swooped around him. His fists were clenched. The wind blew into his face. Yet he stood there like a stone until he had calmed himself, before he went back to the hall.

THEY WENT TO THE ALTHING. Bjarni saw Eirik Arnarson there.

"I heard you had come back, with a new pair of boots, too," Eirik said. He put out his soft ringed hand. "Someone said King William knighted you."

Bjarni laughed. "Why should I kneel to the Red King when I can clasp hands with Eirik Arnarson?"

"I am not sure if that is a compliment. You know that Sigurd Gormsson is here."

"Is he?"

Bjarni looked around him. They were standing near the height of the sloping plain above the lake of Thingvellir, where the Council of Iceland met. A shelf of lava cast its shadow over the green grass behind him. Half the people in Iceland talked and walked among the booths set up along the side of the plain. Eirik pointed to a booth in the row on their left.

"There—in the Vestman Booth. That is where Sigurd is."

Bjarni turned back to the chieftain. "You know that Hoskuld and my brother Ulf robbed me of my inheritance."

Eirik looked troubled. He patted the air with his hands. "That is harshly spoken. Harshly spoken."

Bjarni frowned at him. "It was not kindly done, either."

"I am afraid that nothing can be changed. Hoskuld knew the law. He spoke to the right people—it was all done before witnesses."

"He had no right!"

"Ah, you know, a man may choose not to have his bastards inherit of him."

"Do not call me a bastard, Eirik. He married my mother."

"The old way. By handfast. The Church says that issue of such marriages are bastard." Eirik shrugged his shoulders. "There is no help for it."

Bjarni's blood beat in his ears. He tore his gaze away from Eirik and scanned the plain of Thingvellir again. Another man came toward him and Eirik.

This was Ketil Grettirson, Ketil Longheels he was called.

Like Bjarni he prayed to the gods of the Aesir. He said, "We are having a horse fight later. Will you come?"

"Whose horses?" Eirik said.

Ketil talked of the horse fight. Ulf came up to them. Bjarni had mastered himself; he could smile at his brother.

"You know that your new father-in-law is here."

"Sigurd?" Ulf looked all around him. "Do you think he is here to make trouble with us?"

"Maybe we can get her dowry from him," Bjarni said.

Ulf grunted. He set his hands on his hips. "Let him come to me, if he wants to make peace," he said, in a loud voice. "Eirik! I want a word with you."

He and Eirik wandered away a few steps to talk. Ketil took Bjarni's arm and turned his back to them. He murmured, "I have eight for the sacrifice, will you make nine?"

"Now?" Bjarni glanced around to see they were unheard. "There are hundreds of Christians here. They will squeal like piglets if they find out."

Ketil said, "There are also enough of the old faith here to make up the nine, which is not true elsewhere."

A burst of laughter resounded from Ulf and Eirik. Bjarni lowered his voice. "Are there so few of us left in Iceland that we have to risk outlawry?" He nodded to Ketil. "I will come."

"Good." Ketil clapped his shoulder and went off.

Standing on the Law Rock, the Lawgiver recited the laws of the Republic before anyone who was interested. Bjarni went through the crowded valley toward the booth where Sigurd was staying.

Gudrun's father sat on a stool before a booth roofed in a striped sail. He had a piece of wood in his hand and was whittling on it, but he cut with the blade of the knife held toward himself.

"Cut downward," Bjarni said. "It's good luck."

Sigurd did not look up. He said, "You heathen lump."

"After your meeting with the Bishop, I thought you'd have learned humility. My brother married your daughter. Will you give us her dowry?"

"Is she here?"

"Yes—there across the way."

Sigurd looked off across the Althing. His grey hair had faded to white. "Send her here, let me talk to her. I will give her what she is due." He lifted his head toward Bjarni. "But to her and her husband, not a disinherited bastard." He turned his back on Bjarni.

"Sigurd," Bjarni said to his back, "at Fenby, that was I. I alone." He went off across the stream of people coming up the valley from the lakeside.

He spent the next hour composing a poem and teaching it to three boys. Giving them each a mark, he sent them out around the Althing to recite the poem.

> *Sigurd came to Fenby*
> *With eight longships*
> *Bjarni called Loki*
> *Set him on the beach*
> *Loki thrashed his children on the beach*
> *Sigurd turned his back and ran*
> *From fires and Bjarni on the beach*

After a little while he walked through the gathering again and heard people laughing over the poem, and Sigurd had gone inside his booth.

The Hoskuldssons were staying at Eirik Arnarson's booth. Gudrun sat outside it talking to Andres. Bjarni came around the long side of the booth in time to hear her call to Hiyke to bring her a cup of water.

Hiyke was inside the booth with her sister. "Draw it yourself," she said.

Andres brought Gudrun the cup of water. She was not satisfied with that. In a loud voice, she said, "There is a lazy old woman here who has forgotten she owes the roof over her head to me."

Bjarni went over to her. "Your father is here—he wishes to see you."

Gudrun went off, Andres at her heels like a lapdog. Bjarni went into the booth.

Hiyke's sister was saying, "Is that how it is at Hrafn-fell? Come live with us."

"Hrafnfell is my home," Hiyke said.

Her sister lifted her voice. "Well met, Bjarni Hoskulds-son. It is all over the west of Iceland that you have come back a rich man."

He drew water from the crock in a cup and sat on the bench near Hiyke. "Appearances are deceiving, as Loki said to the Giant's horse."

Hiyke's sister laughed heartily. Hiyke said, "You see he still traffics with demons." She raised her eyes to him. "What had Eirik to say to you?"

"Nothing I wanted to hear."

"Ah," she said. "He is soft, that man, and gentle, and unjust."

Bjarni drank the water in the cup. He sat listening to Hiyke talk to her sister.

BJARNI WENT TO WATCH the horses fighting, and Ulf came up to him.

"Did you spread that scurrilous poem about Sigurd?"

Bjarni had the jug of mead under his arm, and he pulled the stopper out and lifted it to his lips. His brother was very red in the face.

"If you did," Ulf said, "you cost us Gudrun's dowry. Sigurd is a rich man, too."

"We have managed before this without his help," Bjarni said.

"And why did you talk to him? Did I not tell you that we would let him come to us?"

Bjarni held the jug out to him. "Here. You sound un-happy sober."

Ulf looked away. They stood a moment watching the horses maul each other. Bjarni was glad he had bet only a mark on the red stallion, which the dun stallion was driving to its knees. At last Ulf took the jug.

"Listen to me," he said, in a whisper. "If it were up to me, I would never have taken Hrafnfell. I hate the work, you know—it's all work, and no pleasure. Gudrun, now, she has taught me how to take joy in life. But Papa gave me the High Seat."

"I do not blame you for what Hoskuld did," Bjarni said.

Ulf put out his hand and gripped Bjarni's arm. "I know you do not."

"If you continue it, I will blame you."

Ulf's eyes narrowed. Bjarni walked away from him. Behind him a great cheer went up; and a stallion whistled.

The sun sank below the horizon but its light still streamed across the sky. Eirik Arnarson had a suit before the Althing. Bjarni with the rest of his family went to stand behind his chieftain. When Eirik had received the verdict, Bjarni left the others and walked off along the foot of the valley wall. He met eight other men and they climbed up to the top of the wall and walked across the lava flow.

The cold wind blew. The broken surface of the rock was flecked with volcanic glass. Spurs of frozen lava towered up over the men. Ketil Longheels led a horse along by a braided rope, and the others followed him in single file. There were boulders heaped and scattered over the plain. Ash crunched under their feet. They came to a great square rock heaped around with bones.

The nine men made a circle. They passed an old knife from hand to hand. Each as he touched it said the names of the gods. By chance Bjarni was ninth to touch it. He spoke the name of the Thunderer who had preserved him through everything.

He killed the horse. The others helped him cut it up and drag the pieces onto the flat top of the rock. Old bones littered the rock, and he kicked them off. Three ravens circled over him. Another joined them. Another came, and another. Bjarni laid out the flesh of the horse on the rock.

The birds screeched, their wings flapped all around him. They dropped down, tearing at the meat, pecking his blood-covered hands. He climbed down the side of the rock. The other men were kneeling in a circle among the bones. He took his place among them.

The old knife was still in his hand. Once it had killed men to the glory of Thor. He put his head back. He longed to drive the knife into his chest, to give the god his blood. The birds clamored and fought over the horse-flesh. Blood dripped down the side of the rock.

The sun was rising again. One by one the men stirred. Bjarni left the circle and wandered off onto the empty plain to collect himself. The rock was crowded with birds. With the other men he walked back toward Thingvellir.

Ketil came up beside him as they walked. Bjarni said, "This place has not been used for sacrifice in years."

"Maybe not for a century," Ketil said. It had been a hundred years since Iceland turned Christian. He added, "Maybe never again."

"Why did you not ask my brother to join us?"

"Ulf?" Ketil shot a sharp look up at him. "Ulf kisses the Cross now, Bjarni. Did you tell him we were coming here?"

Bjarni shook his head. "Everything has changed." He had guessed at what Ketil told him, but he had not believed it.

"Be careful." Ketil pointed to Bjarni's bloody hands.

"You should wash that off, before anyone else sees you."
He walked away across the lava.

Bjarni hid his hands in his coat. He washed the blood
away in a barrel of rainwater, behind Eirik Arnarson's
booth.

Hiyke was within the booth, kneeling by her chest.
When she saw him, she came to him, and they stood in
the doorway. She said, "Why did you make that poem?
Now Sigurd is paying men to call you a pagan."

"Is he?" Bjarni said.

She had her shawl in her hands, and she lifted it up
over her head and folded the ends over her breast, so that
her face was framed in it. She said, "Be careful. People
are killed, sometimes, for making poems."

"I will make another," he said.

He went off around the Althing, putting the words together, and found men to speak the poem about.

> *Sigurd Green-Tongue*
> *Talks and talks*
> *He talks so much*
> *Grass grows on his tongue*
> *The sun shines*
> *The dew falls*
> *The shit accumulates*
> *The grass grows on his tongue*

That one went around so fast he heard people laughing
over it ahead of him, as he went back to Eirik Arnarson's
booth.

Later there were horse-races on the lower part of the plain. He went there to watch and saw Gudrun and Sigurd standing together, deep in talk. He walked by close enough to let them know that he saw them, and went up on a rusty outcrop of lava to watch the races.

Ulf was still short with him. He could not bear Andres, who fawned on him like a dog now. Gifu was back at Hrafnfell, and Hiyke would not let him alone with her. He drifted by himself through the crowd, or sat in the sun by Arnarson's booth door. In the late afternoon there was a brawl over a law-suit in which many people were involved, and the fighting spread from booth to booth as more and more men took sides. Bjarni kept out of it. He found himself standing near the Law Rock, with the great lava shelf behind him, and Eirik Arnarson and some other men nearby, all trying to avoid the fight.

They shook hands, and someone asked him about the English court. He told them of the richness and idleness of the men around the king, and of the king's great-heartedness.

Eirik said, nervously, "That would make a fine poem, very uplifting."

"Oh, Red William's court is much uplifted," Bjarni said, "nearly all the time. Don't you like my recent poems, Eirik?"

"You are making trouble where none need be," Eirik said. "Here, is that knife of English work?"

He showed Eirik the knife. They talked of England, and the men passed the knife from hand to hand.

One man said, "Is England a fair place, as it says in the old songs?"

"All forest and tilled ground," Bjarni said.

"Bah. There is tilled ground in Iceland, too, but nothing ripens."

Eirik lifted his eyes from the knife. "Is that true?"

One of the other men said, "This year I will have no harvest at all, and I put eighteen bushels of seed into the ground."

Their voices changed, speaking of this; their voices hardened and saddened.

"No one will thresh grain this year. Last year we gathered only a hundred bushels in the whole province. And there was ice in Breidavik until Pentecost, and there is ice in Hvitafjord yet."

"It's the damned horse-eaters," one of them said, "spitting in the face of Christ, so that God blights our land in vengeance."

Bjarni put his dagger back in the sheath. His eyes moved from face to face. The men talked on.

"Did you hear that someone spilled blood for the ravens —here, right here, during the Althing?"

"I can't give credit to it," Eirik said. "They are not so bold."

"They are a curse on us, all over Iceland."

Eirik elbowed the speaker in the side. But the hot words came forth.

"They ought to be hanged, all of them."

Eirik said, "Forebear." He aimed his gaze at Bjarni.

One by one, they remembered; they turned toward him, their faces taut. Bjarni put his hands on his belt.

"Nothing grows in Iceland that you can make rope from, either," he said. "But mark me. When more men spilled blood for the ravens here, we had good harvests in Iceland."

He walked away from them. On the plain, the fighting had stopped, and the bells were pealing for another lawsuit.

THE ALTHING ENDED, and Bjarni and his family went back to Hrafnfell. The sea was flat-calm, and the air warm and gentle, yet Ulf made no mention of taking *Swan* out after the fish. He and Gudrun stayed abed until well into the day.

Gifu rode the grey mare across the hillside. Bjarni had spoken of going with her, but she had put him off. Awhile after she had gone, he saw Kristjan stealing away.

At the corner of the barn, he stood watching his step-brother's dark head hurrying away above the waving grass. He held down his temper. Gifu would do as she wished. Taking the axe, he went up to the woodshed to cut wood.

Late in the day, when the tide was coming in, he drove the sheep in off the rocks where they had been grazing on the seaweed. The sun was shining on the bulging cliff where the ravens nested. On Midsummer's Day the sun rose behind that cliff. He climbed the hillside toward the farm hall. Already the days were shrinking, the sunlight dwindling, and thinking of it he felt something tighten in him. He began to hurry.

Ulf was sitting in the High Seat. He wore a fine shirt stitched with red rosettes. Bjarni sat down on the bench beside him.

"Where have you been finding the fish? We should go out tomorrow, if this weather holds."

Ulf sat forward, looking angry. "I will decide that."

Andres walked in, his heavy feet clomping on the floor. Jon was behind him.

"I will take the ship," Bjarni said, to goad Ulf. "If you don't want to."

"*Swan* is my ship," Ulf said. "This is my farm."

Andres came toward the table. "I agree with Bjarni," he said loudly.

Ulf and Bjarni stared at one another. Roughly, Ulf said, "Don't try to give orders on my farm."

"It should be his farm," Andres said.

"Andres," Bjarni said, "I do not need your help."

Hiyke came into the hall with a basket of bread under her arm. She watched them through the corners of her eyes. Stooping, she put the bread down on the stone of the hearth. The silver cross swung in the air under her chin.

Ulf said, through his teeth, "Do not make me regret that I have let you stay here."

"I will stay here," Bjarni said, "if you let me or no."

Ulf rose and tramped around the table and toward the door. Andres glared across the table at Bjarni.

"There is no being friends with you anymore."

Bjarni spat over the table into the dust of the floor. "That's more of a friend than you are."

Hiyke was taking off her shawl. She said, "Andres, fetch in the milk from the barn."

Obediently he went off. At the door he glowered back at Bjarni, who pretended not to see him. The door slammed.

"Not even the fire can warm this hall," Hiyke said. "Have you seen my son?"

"He is with Gifu," Bjarni said.

She flung up her head. Coming to the edge of the table, she leaned toward him and said, "They went off together?"

"They will come back separately," he said.

"God throttle him."

"It is her doing. With her, everything goes by her measure."

"She is a child," Hiyke said hotly. "And far from her home."

"You judge her poorly if you think she cannot mind herself."

Hiyke sat down on the bench opposite him. She put her elbows on the table and set her chin on her hands.

"She lies, and she steals, which is child's work."

"What has she stolen?"

"A trinket of Gudrun's. Gudrun thinks it is lost—she has not left off nagging me to find it since we came back from Thingvellir."

He put out his hand to her, and promptly she laid her hand in his. He said, "I will handle Gudrun for you."

He raised her hand to kiss it, but she drew back. He let her go. She turned half away from him. He thought she was about to speak, but then the door burst open and Kristjan came in.

She sprang up to her feet. "You lazy, lecherous brat," she cried. She fell on her son, caught him by the nose, and smacked the side of his head so hard Bjarni startled at the sound.

"Mama." Kristjan escaped from her grip. His nose was red.

"Keep away from her," Hiyke cried. "Can you not let her learn to be good?"

Bjarni watched Kristjan circle away from her, avoiding her. The boy blushed. Hiyke gave chase to him, calling him names, and cornered him and struck him again.

Gudrun appeared on the steps. She ran down the length of the hall and pulled Hiyke away from Kristjan. "Leave him alone—your own son!" she cried. "You call yourself Christian!"

"He is my son, to chastise as I wish," Hiyke said.

The two women, one fair and one dark, were nose to nose. Kristjan slid by them out of the corner and ran from the hall. The rest of the family was gathering for supper.

Hiyke cried, "Shall he grow up like you, a slave of pleasure?"

Gudrun crossed herself. "Or like you, passing judgment on others for your own sins?" Straight-backed, she walked away from Hiyke.

Ulf went to his wife and kissed her. Hiyke's face was

suddenly fiery red. She ran up the steps and out of the hall. Bjarni watched her go. Gudrun was near the mark, then.

Ulf slid into the High Seat on Bjarni's left. He said, "Women fight like geese, over nothing."

"Unlike us," Bjarni said.

Ulf grunted. He moved away from Bjarni.

Gifu brought a cheese and a dish of onions into the hall. After her came Hiyke with the meat and fish and the soup. Gudrun sat on the hearth, smoothing down her skirt with her hand. Bjarni had never seen her work. The other women put the meal on the table, and the men sat down to eat.

Gifu sat down beside Bjarni, her hands on the small of her back. She groaned.

"I'm getting fat as a monk."

"What is that?"

She followed his eyes to the front of her dress. Turning out the top of her bodice, she showed him the amber star clipped to her shift. "Isn't it pretty?"

Gudrun was sitting down in the High Seat, beside her husband. Hastily Gifu closed her gown.

"Give it back to her," Bjarni said.

Gifu's eyes narrowed; she shot an evil look at him. Gudrun leaned past Ulf to see them. Gifu said to Bjarni, "Why should I tell you anything?" She glanced at Gudrun. Reluctantly she unfastened the clip and gave it to Ulf's wife.

Gudrun cried out. "My clip!" She showed it to Ulf.

Everyone in the hall turned to look. Gudrun wheeled on Gifu. She leaned forward across her husband as if he were furniture.

"You went through my things! What else did you steal?"

On the far side of the High Seat, Hiyke said, "Remember you are a Christian, Gudrun."

Ulf pushed his wife back into her place. "What kind of a woman have you brought here?" he asked Bjarni.

Bjarni turned toward the food. He pulled a platter to him and began to slice the mutton.

The three women were staring at one another. Gifu said hotly, "Sweet, kindly Gudrun, please forgive me, saint of saints—"

Gudrun said, "You foul-mouthed slut."

"You butterfly-tongue!" Gifu got up from the bench. In a good imitation of Gudrun's swaying, short-stepping walk, she went off down the room. "Oh, Ulf!" Her voice was a squeak. She stroked her hand over her hair, her eyes half-shut. "Pray, saddle the horse. Pray, Hiyke, bring me the milk so I may wash my face. Pray, Gifu, bring me the face so I may wash my milk."

Everyone was laughing, except Gudrun. Even Ulf laughed. Gudrun pulled on his arm.

"Stop her!"

Ulf straightened his face. He winked past her at Bjarni.

"Stop her," Gudrun said, "or sleep with the stock."

Ulf turned away. Gifu had come to Kristjan, sitting at the end of the table, and she leaned down to whisper in his ear. Kristjan stopped smiling. He pushed her away, so that she staggered.

"Gifu," Bjarni said.

Her face turned toward him, her eyes wide with malice. Her hair stood out in fuzzy tendrils like an aura. "Gifu! Gifu!" Up and down the hearth she aped a long-legged, heavy walk that set the others laughing again; Bjarni realized that it was he whom she mocked. His ears burned. Yet he had to laugh. In a deep voice she said, "The King of England would have made me his knight, but I came back to my true-love." She thumped her chest. "The sheep!"

"Be still!" Gudrun shouted at her.

"What offends you?" Hiyke said. "Does she remind you that you are barren?"

Gifu was mimicking Andres now, cajoling and smiling and bowing. Her great belly made her awkward. Ulf turned to Bjarni.

"Stop her. Who knows what she might say?"

Bjarni said, "What are you afraid to hear?"

Another howl of laughter went up from Hiyke and the people watching Gifu. Gudrun stood up in her place. "I will not bear this." She rushed out of the hall. Ulf swore. He left the High Seat to follow her. Bjarni watched him go.

Gifu watched also; she squared her shoulders the way Ulf did, and her mouth opened, full of words.

Bjarni said, "Gifu!"

She turned; she stuck out her chin. He said, "Come and eat."

After a time she did as he said.

When the meal was done and the table cleared, Hiyke went to her loom, and the other people of Hrafnfell found things to do. Bjarni sat at the table and watched Gifu.

She was trying to catch Kristjan's eye. The boy sat with his head bent, his gaze pinned to the ground. Gifu stamped her foot; she cleared her throat, and yet he would not look up. At last she left the hall. As soon as her back was turned, Kristjan raised his eyes to her. But he did not go to seek her. He went to sit by his mother instead.

Ulf had come in again. Bjarni called to him, "Play chess with me."

His brother threw him a wild, angry look and stamped down the hall toward the door into the little room where he and Gudrun slept.

When night had fallen Bjarni crossed the yard to the sleeping booth. It was set back into the hillside; heavy beams of driftwood supported the sod roof. In the middle of the long room a fire burned. Andres and Jon sat on the bed against the right-hand wall, taking their shoes off, when Bjarni came in.

He said, "I am going out to fish tomorrow, if anyone wants to come with me."

His half brothers lifted their heads in unison. "In *Swan*?" Andres said.

"*Swan* is Ulf's ship. I will take one of the boats."

Ulf stalked into the long room. His heavy jaw was thrust out like a codfish's. He came straight up to Bjarni and said, "You let that happen! You let your English whore tease my wife to tears. She is crying now."

"I don't doubt it," Bjarni said.

He stripped off his coat and threw it across the foot of his bed. Ulf got him by the arm and swung him around.

"My advice to you is to get out of here," he said to Bjarni. "Take your slut. You have made bad enemies, and you have outworn my hospitality."

"Your hospitality!" Bjarni shoved him.

"I am warning you," Ulf said. Andres and Jon came around the fire, one to either side of the hearth, their eyes on Bjarni. With the fire at their backs and their faces in shadow they looked wolfish.

"Well, you have warned me," Bjarni said, "but against three of you I think I should have the first blow." He cocked his fist back and drove it forward into Ulf's stomach.

They rushed on him. Under their weight he was borne back, and his spine hit the edge of the bed. He fell onto the bed, got his feet up, and shoved Ulf back away from him. Andres dove onto him as he lay there, and Bjarni rolled over and knocked him away.

Ulf hit him from the side. Bjarni slipped down to one knee. He folded his arms over his head. They pounded at him, their fists bouncing off his arms. A boot came at his chest. He lunged forward to meet it. With the boot in his hands he pushed the body attached to it back toward the hearth.

He managed to stand up. With a lucky hit he knocked Jon away from him, and for a moment he and Ulf milled at each other, taking and giving the hardest blows they could. Ulf stepped back first, blood running down his face from his nose.

Bjarni gasped for breath. None of his brothers was down; they circled him, wary, their fists raised. Their faces gleamed. There was light in the room, more light than before.

Ulf shouted and rushed at Bjarni again, and Jon and Andres came at his back. Bjarni slid his feet along the floor. He fended off Ulf's first round arching blows. Getting his back to the wall, he set himself and began to strike at them all.

They hit him, fists and feet thudding on his body and arms and legs. He took that, glad to take it if he could hit them back. He made them stagger. With a hot joy he realized that he could fight them all at once.

"The bed is burning!"

That was Gifu. Bjarni softened Andres with a hard stroke in the stomach and laid him out on the floor. The jumping light of the fire glistened on Ulf's face. Jon had flinched back. Other people were around them, pulling at them. Bjarni lifted his fists and flung himself on Ulf.

They went down hard. Ulf elbowed him in the throat. He tucked his chin down; he fought for breath. Gifu was screaming his name. The fire blazed down one side of the booth and on the ceiling. She pulled at his arm.

"You will burn—you will burn—"

He lurched to his knees. Ulf rolled onto his back, his face painted with blood that shone brilliant in the firelight. Bjarni got him by the wrist and dragged him toward the door. Ulf got his feet under him. He yanked his arm free and blundered the rest of the way. Bjarni's knees wobbled. He stepped across the threshold into the mist of the night.

The others were standing around at a distance from the fire, watching. Gifu held Bjarni's arm against her side. He turned back toward the heat. The walls of the booth were of lava but the wooden beams, the straw beds, and now even the sod roof were burning.

"What happened?" Ulf said.

Jon was doubled over, his hands on his knees. "I guess —when I hit the fire, I knocked something in. A chair. Something." He snuffled and shook his head, spraying blood around.

Bjarni licked his knuckles. His arms and shoulders hurt.

Hiyke walked in among the men. Her black shawl flapped. She said, "What were you doing, that you did not stop to put out the fire? God's Love, none of you is fit to live here."

None of the men spoke. Over her head, Bjarni met Ulf's eyes. They looked long at one another; something rueful and friendly passed between them. Together they started toward the shed, for tools to keep the fire from spreading.

BJARNI FISHED all the next day in the bay with a handline. In the owl-light, he and Gifu sat on the beach splitting the fish and hanging them to dry.

"What do you think of Hiyke?" he asked her.

"I love her," Gifu said at once.

That startled him; it seemed unlike her. He wiped his knife on the cloth. His sleeves glittered silver with scales.

"She rides her horse with me," Gifu said. "She gave me three dresses. She even likes the baby coming."

"What did she say about you and Kristjan?"

"Oh," Gifu said, without looking up, "I just wanted to see what he was like." Then she said, "It is Hiyke whom you love, isn't it?"

"Yes."

"Anyone you love, I love," she said.

He slit open a white fish-belly. Hiyke was pitting him against his brothers—against Gudrun, in the end. Because of the fight, they had lost the sleeping booth. There was a lesson in that. He remembered the fight, and his heart quickened. He could have beaten them all, if the fire had not interfered.

"What are you thinking about?" Gifu asked.

He started out of his dreams and bent over the fish.

THE NORTH WIND blew clouds over the sky, and they settled on the mountains and hid the pass from sight and shut out the sun. One day a man walked down out of the clouds to Hrafnfell. It was Ketil Longheels. He carried all his possessions on his back.

Bjarni met him in the yard. Ketil shook his hand.

"I have come to warn you," Ketil said. "And to take you with me, if you will go."

"What is this?" Bjarni asked.

Hiyke was in the cookhouse door, watching.

Ketil said, "I have been summoned to my local Thing. I know what it is about. They are going to outlaw us. The nine of us who sacrificed at Thingvellir."

His voice was low, yet Bjarni knew Hiyke had overheard him. He did not look at her. Ketil's face was white with strain. Bjarni took his arm.

"Come into the hall."

They went down the steps and along the room to the table. Bjarni brought over the jug. They sat down with the jug between them on the table. They were alone in the hall, but the little door at the end stood ajar, the door to Ulf's and Gudrun's room.

"I am leaving Iceland," Ketil said. "I know what will happen. There is nothing to be done about it—and I would only humiliate my family if I stayed."

"Drink," Bjarni said.

They each drank of the mead. Ketil could not keep still; as he spoke, his hands twitched and turned in half-finished gestures.

"There must be a place a man can go. You have been all over the world. Come with me."

"No one has summoned me yet," Bjarni said.

"They will. They know all our names—it was all about at the Thing; you must have noticed." Ketil wiped his hand over his face. "There is no keeping secrets at the Althing."

"What of your wife?" Bjarni asked.

Ketil put his head down on his hands. After a moment he straightened again. His face was an old man's face. "She shut the door on me."

Through his shirt Bjarni touched the amulet around his neck. Here was another strange twist in his fate.

"Will you come?" Ketil said.

Bjarni shook his head. "I will not leave Hrafnfell."

"You will be outlawed."

"Yet I will not leave Hrafnfell. You can stay here until you are ready to go on—stay here and rest."

Ketil lifted the jug to his lips. Bjarni left him there, already half-drunk.

He found Hiyke in the shed, milking the goats. She held one goat's head and shoulders between her knees and bent over its back to reach its bag.

"Ketil will stay with us a few days," Bjarni said.

"He is welcome," she said. Her hands worked rhythmically. "You were one of them. At the famous sacrifice at Thingvellir."

"Yes."

"What a fool you are sometimes."

The goat bleated, protesting. Hiyke straightened and moved the bucket, and the goat backed out of the grip of her legs. Bjarni leaned against the ladder. He put his hands behind him on the smooth wood of the rung.

"Does it matter to you? You lived so long with Hoskuld —it cannot make such a difference to you as it does to the others."

She stroked her fingers over her face. Deep creases framed the corners of her mouth. She reached for the pail.

"Leave it," he said. "Answer me."

"I don't know," she said. "I don't know what I think, since Hoskuld died."

"Did you love him?"

"Yes."

"Why did you never marry?"

"He would not go into a church," she said, "and I would not sit in the High Seat and take the hammer on my knees."

With a sharp sideways motion of her head she dismissed that. She said, "What about this news that Ketil brings? Does anyone else know that you were there also?"

"Probably. I must be summoned to our Thing before they can judge me. I can guard against that."

She was staring at him, her wide-set eyes like crystals. "How long can you stand against the whole of Iceland?"

"You are making more of it than there is." He picked up the pails of milk and started toward the door. "It will fade. Next year no one will remember; there will be some other scandal." He took the milk across the yard toward the cookhouse.

KETIL STAYED only that one night at Hrafnfell, and he slept so restlessly that Bjarni, who was sleeping near him in the hall, wakened three or four times in the night. Just after dawn Ketil walked along the road around the bay.

Bjarni went with him. They came to the place on the cliff where the path met the sea-road. A bitter wind was blowing from the north and heavy clouds hung low above them.

"Be careful," Ketil said. "Maybe I imagine it, but I see nothing but trouble for you with your family."

Bjarni gave him some money. "You may need this," he said. "Go to Eirik Arnarson, he is always outfitting ships, and he will give you an oar to pull, to Norway or Greenland perhaps."

"Thank you. Once more I will ask you to go with me."

"I will not run," Bjarni said.

"You make me ashamed," Ketil said, "and at this point, if this were an old tale, I would stay and help you, but I am going on." He shook Bjarni's hand a long time and went away down the road.

Bjarni went the other way, down to the beach. The sea was crashing against the shore; the wind stung his cheek. He blinked into the wind, looking out to sea. The waves heaved and bashed their heads together under manes of foam. The spray flew over the rocks. Exhilarated, he opened his mouth and filled his lungs with the storm wind. He spread out his arms. When the storm reached Iceland, these waves would batter at the cliff behind him. Nothing could match them except the great whales, who played with storms. Bjarni shouted. He called out old chants in honor of the storm to come. His face pebbled with salt water, and his spirits high, he walked back up the cliff road toward Hrafnfell.

THE STORM BROKE over them. Day after day sleet and rain swept in along the wind, hammering the grass down and roaring around the houses so loud that sometimes the people inside could not hear one another talk. The blackened pit of the burned-out sleeping booth filled with water and floating char. The rain running down the hill began to seep into the barn, and Bjarni took the pick and the shovel and ditched along the outside of the wall to lead the water off. Half-frozen, he went to the cookhouse, took off his wet clothes, and sat down in the warmth behind the oven with the jug of mead.

Gudrun came into the cookhouse.

"Oh," she said. "I thought to find Hiyke here."

Bjarni was sitting half-naked on the stool, his feet propped against the wall; he pulled his shirt across his lap. Gudrun held her hands behind her. She smiled at him.

"I don't know where Hiyke is," he said.

"Oh, well," Gudrun said. "It was unimportant." She came a step closer to him. "My father hates you worse than the Bishop," she said, "which is a thing to marvel at, you know." Her skirt grazed his fingers.

Gifu pushed in the door. She saw them together, and she grinned wide as a fox.

Gudrun had turned and was taking down pots from the shelf. "Have you seen Hiyke?" she said.

"She is in the loft," Gifu said.

Gudrun went out with an armload of pots.

"All women are sisters," Gifu said. She perched herself on the bench beside him, her arms around her ripening body.

Bjarni took a long pull on the jug. "Forget you saw that."

"Never," Gifu said.

A booming gust of the wind thundered on the sod roof like a great fist, and all the ladles and spoons hanging from the beams danced on their hooks. Gifu shrank down.

"When will it stop? It just goes on and on—"

"Another three or four days, at the most," he said.

"Oh."

He touched her neck with his fingertips. "It will pass."

The storm was a blessing to him. By law he had to be summoned to the Thing by the man bringing suit against him. Fortunately, he had no legal home; he was just a guest at Hrafnfell. Therefore the summoner had to give him the summons to his face, and before witnesses. As long as he kept away from suspect people, he would be safe from the law. While the storm raged, no one would take to the road to come to Hrafnfell.

"She looked at you like a rat at cheese," Gifu said.

Bjarni pinched her neck. "Keep it to yourself, or I'll thrash you."

"Oh, Bear."

.   .   .

THE STORM DIED AWAY. The sun rose brilliant in a cloudless sky. The windward sides of all the buildings at Hrafnfell were coated with a shell of ice, which melted in an hour. Gudrun Sigurdsdottir rode away around the bay, to hear Mass said at Eirik Arnarson's church. The following day, Bjarni and his brothers set about cleaning up the mess of the burned sleeping booth.

The rain had soaked the ashes and char to a black paste. Bjarni and Ulf waded in up to their knees and shoveled the sludge into the cart. In the back of the booth, where the room was cut deeply into the hillside, Bjarni found the heavy filigree clasp of the coat King William had given him.

"You should have stayed there," Ulf said, "where you were welcome."

Bjarni shined the face of the blackened clasp with his thumb. "It was not my home."

"I am asking you one final time to give up your claim to the farm," Ulf said.

Bjarni straightened; his brother's voice warned him. The walls of the booth reached up above the level of his head. On his left, Andres suddenly appeared, standing on top of the wall, a rake on his shoulder. Bjarni glanced behind him and saw Jon there.

"Yes," he said to Ulf. "Go on."

Ulf bit his lip. He raised the shovel in both hands. Loudly he said, "Bjarni Hoskuldsson, I summon you to the Smoke River Thing, to let it be judged that you adored false gods, which is against the law in Iceland."

His voice cracked. He gathered breath again. "I do this in pursuit of a case I bring against you, as head of your family."

With an effort Bjarni kept his hands at his sides. "Are you sure that the words are right?" he asked.

"Gudrun had them of Eirik Arnarson himself, only yesterday," Ulf said.

Bjarni stirred, lifting his arms. Ulf quickly clambered up to the top of the wall. He still carried the shovel. Bjarni looked up at his brothers, ranged around him on the walls, and each had some weapon.

"You cannot unsay it now," he said to Ulf. "But I warn you that you have made this a different fight, threatening me with weapons." He walked out of the foul pit of the sleeping booth.

ALL THE REST of the day he walked on the cliff over the sea, trying to sort out his thoughts. If he stood before the people at the Thing, he would not lie, he would not deny his faith, and they would outlaw him. He could leave Iceland, or he could stay, but if he stayed anyone could kill him. He climbed down the cliff to the beach. The storm had strewn the sand with driftwood, the bones of the sea.

He sat on the sand and watched the sea. Over his head ravens swooped and chased one another. It was cold and he began to shiver. At last when he was too cold to think he went back up the cliff and crossed the hillside toward his home.

The bulging cliff glittered in the sun, still wet from the storm. A motion at its foot caught his eye. A horse galloped out of the shadow of the cliff and headed toward him. He stopped. It was Hiyke. She rode straight to him and drew rein.

"What will you do now?" she asked. "Do you still think I am making too much of this?"

"No, you are right," he said; he was angry at her for railing at him. "Does that make you proud?"

She lifted the black arches of her brows. The horse snorted and lowered its head. She said, "What will you do?"

He scanned the farmyard, on the slope below him. There was no sign of Ulf. Kristjan loitered in the cookhouse door. The wind played in the grass. There were clouds moving in again from the north. Far down the sky, he saw a flight of geese going south.

He remembered what he had done at Sigurd's church. He said, "Perhaps I can keep them from going to the Thing. If none of us appears, there is no case."

Hiyke nudged the horse with her heel, and it sidestepped closer to him. She said, "That is too dangerous. They'll fight—someone might die. Then there will be no reconciling any of you."

"What would you have me do?"

"Go to the Thing—offer Ulf a fine of some sort."

"I would have to forswear the Aesir," he said.

"Do it, then!"

"No."

"You must. It is the only way."

"No, there is my way."

"To fight."

"To meet them face to face."

Her breath hissed between her teeth. She swiveled her head, looking away from him. Her fists were clenched together over the reins. He put his hand over her two fists. Her hands were cold.

"I am not Kristjan," he said. "You cannot drive me here and there, like a sheep."

She turned her blue eyes toward him again. "Bah. You are as ham-headed as your father."

His temper rose again. He gripped her hands tight. "We made a bargain, which I will honor. All you need do is keep your part of it."

"Damn you," she said, "I will do as I please! As for you, since you came back from England you have lorded it over everybody. You, who have nothing!"

Her eyes were shining. She was half in tears.

He freed her hands. "I did not mean to make you cry," he said.

"I am not crying. It is the wind."

They stood there for a few moments, unspeaking, while she arranged herself again. Finally, she said, "I am a shrew. You have made a bad bargain."

He kissed her mouth. She laid her arms over his shoulders and her lips parted and her breath warmed his tongue.

He was first to draw back. Her eyes were still brimming with tears. She touched his cheek with her fingers.

"I will help you," she said. "Whatever you say, I will do."

"Come home with me."

They went down the steep slope toward Hrafnfell.

WITH THE SLEEPING BOOTH BURNED, everyone except Hiyke and Gifu slept in the hall. There were eight days remaining before the family should go to the Thing. Bjarni kept to himself; he spoke mildly to his brothers when he had to deal with them. Twice he went down to the beach and brought back long beams of driftwood. At night when the others slept, he shaped them into bars. He said charms over them and cut runes on them. The night before the family was to go, while everyone slept, he fitted the bars over the door to the hall and the window in the roof over Ulf's and Gudrun's bed, and there he kept his brothers, for three days, letting only Gudrun go in and out to feed them.

ON THE FOURTH DAY he took down the bars, and one at a time his brothers came out of the hall.

None of them spoke to him. Jon and Andres went away, each in his own direction. The weather was fine; Bjarni took the scythe out to the lower hayfield and began to mow down the hay. After a time, Kristjan joined him with a rake, and they went up and down through the hay.

In the evening they walked down the slope and along the foot of the Raven Cliff. The sun was down, and streaks of purple rimmed the horizon.

Kristjan said, "Why did you pen me in? I have nothing to do with your quarrels."

Bjarni said nothing. The slope fell off steeply toward the hall, so that he stepped down more than he moved forward. Hiyke had bade him lock Kristjan in; she worried that Ulf and the others might attack him if he seemed to side with Bjarni.

"Does Gifu ever talk about me?" the boy said.

"Leave her alone."

"I did nothing to her she did not want."

"*Not,* and *nothing*—" Bjarni stopped; he gripped his stepbrother's arm and made him stand. "That's all you care about, is it? What you do not do? Listen to me, I have some good advice for you. Leave your mother."

"Leave her! But I love her. And where should I go?"

Bjarni started off again down the slope. The scythe lay on his shoulder. "Anywhere but here, or you will be a greyheaded child." He stretched his legs out, walking away from Kristjan.

When he came into the yard, through the opening between the shed and the burned-out sleeping booth, Gifu was standing in the dirt, shouting through the hall door.

"Bring it yourself!"

Gudrun rushed out of the hall. Her skirts billowed and swung around her heels.

"That is my thanks for trying to teach you woman-liness!"

Gifu scurried away from her. "Hag," she cried.

Bjarni went into the shed and hung the scythe on the rafter. Through the door he heard the women trading insults at each other.

He could see Gudrun standing on the threshold of the hall. "You slut," she called.

"Slut, am I? Were you so pious spying on Bear when he was naked, that day in the cookhouse?"

Bjarni went into the yard. Gifu saw him coming and lumbered toward the barn, her hand bracing her back. He pushed her ahead of him into the barn.

The barn was warm and smelled of goats and milk; the goats were gathered in the dark at the far end. Bjarni turned Gifu around to face him.

"I told you not to speak of that."

"It's true," she cried. "She looked on you with such a lust—she wanted you."

The goats bleated, stirring, and Ulf came through them, from the back of the barn. He passed Bjarni without paus-ing. All Bjarni saw of his face were the points of light glowing in his eyes. The door screed on its hinges. Ulf went out.

"Aaaah—" Angry, Bjarni lifted his hand to strike Gifu.

"It is true," she said. "Better he knows it now."

He lowered his hand without touching her.

.   .   .

BEFORE SUNRISE he went back to the hayfield to cut down the rest of the hay. It all had to be brought in before the next rain; he prized the day's sunshine and worked hard. Gifu brought him his dinner at noon. She sat down on a stone at the edge of the field and began to eat his meal for him.

"Hiyke says that Ulf and Gudrun argued all night long."

Bjarni sat down with the scythe to hone it. It was Hoskuld's hone, and his name was marked on it; Bjarni covered that part with his hand. Gifu had eaten his dinner, even the mead. Her chin was covered with crumbs. She leaned back on her braced arms. Her vast belly kept her from sitting upright.

"I will name him after you," she said.

"I have the feeling it is a girl."

"No—it will be a boy, and I will name him Bear."

"Half Iceland already thinks it is my child. Besides, it's unlucky to name a baby for a living person."

"I'll pretend it's for someone else," she said.

She shook the crumbs from her skirt. Bjarni went out again to cut the last of the hay.

Late in the day, all the people of Hrafnfell gathered in the hall for supper. Gifu huddled by the fire. Her face was pinched. Bjarni picked up her hand and found it hot and dry with fever.

"You should go to bed," he said.

She shook her head. Her wild hair drooped on either side of her face; she rubbed her eyes.

At supper she took no food at all. She sat beside him on

the bench and he tried to give her pieces of his meat but she refused. Suddenly she doubled over. Bjarni lifted her in his arms, her legs trailing down. Her hands pushed and tugged on her belly.

The others stood in their places to see. Ulf called, "What is wrong?" Hiyke hurried around the table and laid her thin hand against Gifu's cheek.

"Is she having the baby?" Bjarni said.

"It's too soon. She is fevered. Bring her to bed."

Gifu whimpered. Her eyes closed. Bjarni wrapped her in his coat and took her to the barn. He climbed the ladder with her tucked in one arm. Hiyke went ahead of him to smooth the bed cover and he laid Gifu with her head on the down pillow.

Hiyke brought her a cup of milk steeped with herbs. Gifu's breath was harsh.

She said, "I am poisoned."

Bjarni lifted her up again into his arms. Hiyke sat before him, her silver cross in her fingers.

"Gudrun has poisoned me," Gifu said.

Bjarni and Hiyke looked at one another; they each saw that they agreed.

The girl said no more. Bjarni rocked her, and Hiyke knelt by the bed and prayed. Night came. The barn creaked; the earth had quaked a little. Bjarni felt only a momentary tremble. Just before midnight, Gifu died.

Hiyke pulled her shawl over her head and covered her face with it. Bjarni went down the ladder to the barn.

When he went out the door, Kristjan was standing there. He said softly, "Is she any better?"

Bjarni said, "She is dead."

Kristjan turned away from him. Bjarni put his head back, looking into the starry arch of the sky.

He could not bury Gifu in the mud, in a hole scraped out of the ground. On the hill above the woodyard, he laid out stones in the shape of a longship, pointing the bow north. The wind blew up a rain storm and in the rain he laid Gifu down on her back in the ship and put around her the things she had liked, her favorite clothes, her ribbons. He took the silver amulet from around his neck and laid it beside her. He piled the rocks over her until the whole of the ship was heaped with rock, streaming in the rain.

When he turned away from the grave Hiyke was there behind him on the grey mare. Rain dripped from the horse's mane. Bjarni stood without moving, spiritless, his back to the grave. He stirred himself; putting one foot before the other he started down the hillside, following a sheep-path. Hiyke turned to ride beside him.

Halfway down to Hrafnfell they passed Kristjan, walking up the path. He went by them without saying a word, without even glancing at them. Bjarni looked back and saw the boy kneel down by the ship-mound.

Hiyke said, "Well, what shall we do? We cannot summon Gudrun to the Thing, not now."

The rain was beating into Bjarni's face. He walked with his head down. Above them the sheep were huddled beneath the overhanging Raven Cliff. He glanced back again and saw Kristjan still praying over Gifu.

"We have to kill her," he said.

"You say it so easily."

"Saying it is not doing it."

"It is awful, even to think of it."

"Can we do anything else?"

They were almost in among the farm buildings, and Hiyke pressed her lips together and did not speak. She slid down from the saddle. The yard was deep in mud. They led the horse between them into the barn and Bjarni stripped the harness off. Neither of them spoke. He looked several times at Hiyke as he unsaddled the horse and rubbed it down, but Hiyke's eyes were always downcast.

Later when the rain slackened, Ulf and Gudrun went over the hill to the hot spring. Bjarni went into their room and searched the two chests that stood against the walls, where his brother's wife kept her clothes and goods. In a bottom drawer he found a blue vial, half full of a dust. This he took away with him.

He fed a bit of the dust to a goose, and the goose died.

Hiyke was in the cookhouse. She had lit two hanging lamps against the gloom and was kneading the bread. He passed through the smell of yeast to the bench by the oven.

"I have found the poison," he said.

Hiyke's strong arms pumped in the dough. She had rolled her sleeves up out of the flour and her skin was powdery with it. She did not cease working.

"She is guilty. We both know it, Gifu knew it," she said.

"Then we will kill her," Bjarni said.

Hiyke cast a swift oblique look at him. She rested her hands on the floury board before her. "How?"

"It is a very serious crime," he said. "To kill in secret. You know that."

"It is justice," she said, and gave him another, longer look.

He put the vial of poison on the table. "Give her the poison she gave Gifu."

Her face was like stone. She picked up the vial, looked at it, turned it over in her fingers, and put it away inside her clothes. She went back to kneading the bread.

"I wonder how long she has had it," she said.

"Sigurd gave it to her, at the Althing."

"She had it before then. She came here with it. From the moment she came here, Hoskuld waned."

He did not reply to that, although he knew it was untrue. It rubbed him that she should still think so much on Hoskuld.

THAT EVENING Gudrun did not come to supper. Ulf said, "Maybe she has something already in the oven," and clapped his palm over his belly. His smile was stiff and false. Jon sat by the fire, carving pins out of wood to fasten the rafters of the new sleeping booth. Andres lay down in the dark at the back of the hall and pretended to sleep.

In the morning Bjarni went to the woodyard to cut wood. There was rain coming down. Ulf and Jon came after him to gather logs for the fire. When Bjarni turned his back, they attacked him with knives.

Bjarni swung the axe around and struck the weapon from Jon's hand. Ulf lunged at him and the glittering knife passed between his arm and his body and sliced the shirt on both sides. Bjarni's fingers closed on his brother's wrist. Ulf twisted; he drove the knife into Bjarni's arm. Going down on one knee, Bjarni freed him, and he and Jon ran out of the woodshed.

Bjarni sat down heavily; his hand was running dark with blood pouring down his arm under his sleeve. His head whirled. He dragged the air deep into his lungs. When he was steady again, he put his feet under him and went out of the shed.

The rain had stopped. Low clouds still hid the sky and pressed down over the mountains. Taking the axe in his hand, he went down the slope to the farmyard and let himself into the barn.

Hiyke put her head over the edge of the loft. "Bjarni?"

"I am here," he said, breathless.

She climbed down the ladder, her skirt flapping around her feet. "What happened?" She grasped his arm and held it so that she could pull his sleeve open.

"Ulf and Jon," he said.

"Did you kill them?"

"They ran away."

She bent his arm up to slow the bleeding and climbed the ladder again. Within a moment she was back, a sheet of linen over her arm and a jar in her hand.

"Where did they go?"

He shook his head. The shock of the wound was passing and he felt stronger. She pushed his sleeve up and bathed the long wound in the potion from the jar and wrapped it with the linen.

"I will help you," she said. "You can't fight them all at once."

"Stay here and keep out of this," he said. He turned her face up, his hand on her chin, and kissed her. A sound from the door startled them both.

Kristjan came through the door. He said, "Jon and Ulf are in the hall—Ulf has the sword down off the wall."

Bjarni took the axe by the throat. "Stay here with him," he said to Hiyke, and went out of the barn.

The geese were spread across the yard, grubbing in the mud. Bjarni stood a moment in the doorway of the barn. The door to the hall was open. Within it was no sound, and nothing moved. Bjarni went around the hall to the far side and climbed onto the roof above the bedchamber behind the hall.

He slit the gutskin window with his knife and dropped down through it into the darkened room where Gudrun lay. Quietly he went out to the hall.

Ulf and Jon framed the doorway. Ulf had the broadsword their grandfather had carried and Jon had the hayfork. They did not see Bjarni behind them. He went to the High Seat and sat down in it; he threw the axe onto the table before him.

His half brothers jumped like hares. They sprang away

from the door, spinning to face him. When he saw Bjarni there, Jon cried out.

Bjarni looked from Ulf to Jon. He said, "The rain is passed. We will sail out tomorrow to fish." He stared at Jon. "Go down the valley and bring back as many as will sail with us."

Jon glanced at Ulf, who said nothing.

"Put away the hayfork," Bjarni said, "before you drop it on your foot, and go."

Silently Jon leaned the fork up against the wall and went out of the hall. Bjarni sat back in the High Seat. He had never sat in it before. Now Hiyke and he would share it. Ulf was watching him. His head was lowered, like a hostile dog.

"Go make the ship ready," Bjarni said. He lifted his voice. "Andres! Go with him."

From the back of the room came Andres, stoop-shouldered, who passed by Ulf close enough to touch him before climbing the three steps to the door. As he went out, Hiyke appeared on the threshold.

Ulf sank down slowly onto his heels and laid the sword on the floor. He backed away from it. He said, "I want to stay with Gudrun."

"Do as I told you," Bjarni said.

Ulf raised his hands. "She is dying!" He shook his hands at Bjarni. "You did that to her, didn't you."

"She killed Gifu," Bjarni said. Hiyke was watching them from the doorway.

"I killed Gifu!" Ulf said. "I meant to poison you—I poisoned the mead. She drank it, the greedy slut—"

Bjarni stood up out of the High Seat; he put one foot in the middle of the table and leapt on his brother. He bore Ulf down under him on the floor.

"Stop!" Hiyke pulled his arm. Her strength was nothing, a feather against him. With his hands on Ulf's throat, he let her draw him away. Ulf choked and gasped on the floor.

"You heard him," Hiyke said. "She was innocent! She was innocent—"

Bjarni kicked at Ulf, who scuttled away toward the door.

"She was innocent," Hiyke said. "We killed an innocent woman—"

The door slammed. They were alone in the hall. Bjarni grasped her hands tight in his.

"Listen to me. No one knows you had anything to do with it. Keep still, and no one ever will."

Her eyes widened. "Do you think that is all that matters? I know—I am guilty before God." She scrubbed the back of her hand over her mouth. "You did this to me," she said.

"Ulf will suffer—that is what matters to me. For the rest, keep still."

The sword was lying on the floor a little way from him. He picked it up and carried it to its place on the wall behind the High Seat. He pulled the bearskin off the back of the High Seat.

Hiyke watched him; her face was slack.

He ran his hand over the carved back of the High Seat. The thousands of coils of the Midgard Serpent circled around and around the two posts and the sides. In the middle of the back was carved a scene in relief of two men fishing from a boat. It was Thor, fishing for the World Snake. The flat surfaces of the wood were polished from the skin that had hidden them so long. He ran his fingertips over them, pleased to have uncovered them again. When he looked up Hiyke was gone.

GUDRUN DIED in the night. Bjarni sent Kristjan around the bay to the church to bring back the priest so that Gudrun could be buried. The day passed, and Kristjan did not return.

Bjarni was sitting in the High Seat. Hiyke came to him.

"Where is my son?"

"Probably he spent the night with Eirik," Bjarni said. "There is no hurry."

She seemed much older, and as beautiful as a Norn who kept the world young. He put out his hand to her, where she stood beside his chair.

"Come sit beside me."

"No," she said, loudly.

"You made a bargain with me. I have taken the High Seat, and now you must give me what I desire."

"It was a bargain made in Hell," she said. "I will not honor it, now or ever."

"You are talking out of fear," he said. "If Gudrun did not poison Gifu, certainly she knew."

She took the silver cross in her hand. "My choice is between you and God. After what I have done, only God can save me."

He pinned her with his gaze. "I am giving you no choice," he said. "I will have what I want, no matter what the cost."

"Damn you," she said, "and damn the devil in you."

She looked at him like an enemy. He rubbed his hand over the arm of the serpent chair. That made it easy: he could master enemies.

He said, "Is there any left of that poison?"

"Yes," she said.

He stretched out his hand. "Give it to me."

Her face tightened.

"Give it to me!"

She took the vial from her apron and put it into his hand. He sat back in the High Seat, and she walked out of the hall.

KRISTJAN DID NOT COME BACK the following day, either, but on the day after that, he appeared on the road to Hrafnfell. Two men were riding with him, the priest and Eirik Arnarson himself.

Bjarni saw them from the yard. Going into the hall, he found his brothers sitting in a pack beside the hearth. He stood looking down on them, and none of them would meet his look.

"Kristjan is bringing Eirik Arnarson," he said. "He clearly has been this long telling him what has been happening here and convincing him to interfere. You must all do as I say, or we will be in great trouble."

"You are the cause of it," said Ulf, in a ragged voice.

"I will cause enough for us all if you do not do as I say. You must tell Eirik that you have considered and you are giving up your claim to Hrafnfell to me."

Ulf swiveled his head away. At the far end of the hall the steps creaked.

Hiyke called, "Here is Kristjan."

Bjarni nudged Ulf with his foot. "We will meet them in the yard."

None of his brothers moved. Their shoulders stooped, their heads bowed, they sat like stones on the hearth. Bjarni kicked Ulf, and all three of them sprang up. They went hastily toward the yard.

Hiyke stood on the threshold. She stepped aside to let them pass. Ulf and Jon and Andres went by her. Bjarni took her arm and held her still.

"What will you say to Eirik Arnarson?" he asked.

She swept him with a look as blank as if she were blind. He saw she meant to escape from him if she could.

He tightened his grip on her arm. Low, he said into her ear, "If you are tempted to betray me again, just remember, it was you who poisoned Gudrun Sigurdsdottir."

She gave a violent start. He went away from her, across the yard, to meet Eirik Arnarson.

The chieftain wore a strained smile. He did not offer

Bjarni his hand. He said, "Kristjan here speaks of bad feeling among you, he says you are all fighting."

Kristjan watched from the back of his horse, his face impassive.

"No longer," Bjarni said. "Ulf will tell you."

Ulf raised his head. He pushed back his shaggy fair hair. Flatly he said, "Bjarni is master here. I have given my place in the inheritance to him."

"This is interesting news," Eirik said. He looked from one to the next of the Hoskuldssons. "Is it of your own will?"

Ulf muttered, "Yes."

Now Eirik was staring at Bjarni. "Yet Kristjan here would have it there was force used."

"He is set against me," Bjarni said. "He hates me because I am to marry his mother."

Eirik rubbed his jaw. His eyes glided back toward Kristjan.

"He is lying," the boy said.

The chieftain said, "Hiyke, what is the truth?"

She did not respond.

Kristjan said, "Mother, tell them the truth."

Still she was silent. Her face was like bone, her eyes like two holes burned into bone.

"Mother," Kristjan said. "He will send me away."

Bjarni went to stand by Kristjan's horse. He said, "Answer them, Hiyke."

She raised her glittering eyes. "It is as Bjarni says." She went down into the hall, and the door shut behind her.

Eirik's pent breath exploded from him in a grunt. He said, "I see there is no work for me here." He lifted his reins to go.

Bjarni said to Kristjan, "Get out. If you ever come back, I will give you to the ravens."

Kristjan turned his horse and trotted away after Eirik Arnarson.

LATE IN THE DAY Bjarni went out to the cliff above the sea, where he had carved runes before. In the soft volcanic rock he cut Gifu's name in letters as large as his hand.

> *Ringbearer-no-wife*
> *Thief of my peace*

He could not finish the poem.

In the stone he found runes of Hoskuld's, charms for fishing, charms against ghosts. He found a love-charm with Hiyke's name inside it. He touched the edge of her name. Since she had broken faith with him, he could not think of her without anger.

He sat remembering his father, who had loved no one and trusted no one.

He walked back toward Hrafnfell with the light of the setting sun streaming at his back. His shadow stretched a hundred feet ahead of him over the grass. The grass rippled in waves all across the hillside. Two ravens circled in the sky above the hall of Hrafnfell. He foresaw his doom there, as his father had been doomed. Yet he would not turn aside. Already his shadow had reached the hall. He went into the hall and sat down in the High Seat.

A NOTE ON THE TYPE

This book was set on the Linotype in Granjon, a type named in compliment to Robert Granjon, type cutter and printer—in Antwerp, Lyons, Rome, Paris—active from 1523 to 1590. Granjon, the boldest and most original designer of his time, was one of the first to practice the trade of type founder apart from that of printer.

Linotype Granjon was designed by George W. Jones, who based his drawings on a face used by Claude Garamond (1510–1561) in his beautiful French books. Granjon more closely resembles Garamond's own type than do any of the various modern faces that bear his name.

The book was composed, printed, and bound by American Book–Stratford Press, Inc., Brattleboro, Vermont, and designed by Joy Chu.